Model
PERFECT
PASSION

melanie schuster

KIMANI PRESS™

ISBN-13: 978-0-373-86061-6
ISBN-10:   0-373-86061-7

MODEL PERFECT PASSION

Copyright © 2008 by Melanie Schuster

www.kimanipress.com

Printed in U.S.A.

Dear Reader,

Sometimes when you're not looking for it, love will find you. That's what happens to Billie Phillips and Jason Wainwright. Neither one of them was looking for a serious relationship, but they got one.

Jason didn't make a good impression on Billie when they first met because he viewed her in terms of her physical appearance only. Billie realized that and resented it highly. It took a minute for each of them to set aside their initial assessment of the other and begin to get to know the real person behind the facade. Once they were able to do that, they began to realize that theirs could be a real love, a love to last for all time.

How many of us have judged someone unfairly in the beginning and never gave them a chance to reveal their real personality? And how many times have you been totally caught off guard when a person you thought you couldn't stand turned out to be a fascinating individual? It's happened to me, and that's what gave me the inspiration for this story. Two people who think they know all there is to know about the other person end up getting surprised by love when they open their minds and their hearts.

Stay Blessed,

Melanie

I Chronicles 4:10
MelanieAuthor@aol.com
P.O. Box 5176
Saginaw, Michigan 48638

Dedicated to all my loyal readers.
Thanks for going on another journey with me.

Acknowledgment

A very special thank-you to Rhodora, Phil,
Liz (aka Vlad the Impaler) and Carrie. A special
thank-you to Betty Dowdell, even though thank you
is never enough. Thanks to all the ladies in my group
for keeping me lifted up.

And as always, to Jamil. You're my rock.

Chapter 1

"Is that a dead rat?"

"Yeah, that's a big ol' dead rat. Or a small dead cat. It's kinda hard to say at this point."

The first voice, which belonged to Billie Phillips, was undeniably female, although she sounded like an excited preadolescent boy at the moment. "That's really gross! That was one big-A rat," she said with a whistle. "What else are we going to find?"

The second voice was the deep, amused one of her brother-in-law, Nick Hunter. "This house has been empty for a long time, so we're liable to find

rats, cats, possums, bats and a bunch of drug para-
phernalia. Just watch where you step," he cautioned.

They were looking over a house that she des-
perately wanted to buy. It was a three-bedroom
brick bungalow in a part of Chicago that had seen
better days. The house had fared much worse
than the neighborhood, however. It had passed
through many owners and tenants and it was cur-
rently a mess. It was by far the worst house on the
block and there was a lot of work to be done to it
to make it livable, which was why Billie wanted
to get her hands on it. She'd been working with
Nick at his construction business for over three
months and she was eager to take on more re-
sponsibilities. Nick was mostly into commercial
construction, but he did do some residential work.
That was where Billie's main interest lay and she
was dying to get hold of a house like this. Her
passion was home renovation, and as she'd been
telling Nick, there was no better way to learn the
business of flipping houses than by actually
flipping one. And this semidilapidated house was
just the place to begin, she thought.

Billie's eyes were shining with anticipation
and her face was flushed with pleasure as she
carefully followed Nick's lead in exploring the

deplorable house. Despite wearing jeans, construction boots, a thermal undershirt and a plaid
flannel shirt with a parka on top, she looked
adorable. Nick glanced at her and laughed.

She looked at him quizzically. "What's so
funny?"

"You," he told her. "You've got soot on your
nose, dirt on your jeans and cobwebs in your hair.
You sure don't look like a big-time international
model now," he teased her.

Billie wrinkled her nose at him. "That's
because I'm not. I have a few shoots left to fulfill
a couple of contracts, but after that I'm done with
prowling the runway and tooting my booty up in
the air to show off some ridiculously priced shoes
or whatever," she said, and then grunted as she
used a crowbar to pull up the floor tile in the
bathroom. Nick had shown her how to look for
mold and water damage and she was going after
it like rat terrier.

"I liked modeling—it was fun. But I was doing
it for the money and for no other reason. This is
what I want to do, Nick. I want to take old houses
and make them wonderful again. Oh, dang, is
that mold I smell?" She straightened up from her
semicrouched position and took a good long sniff.

"Cat pee, more like," was his laconic answer. "You might have a diamond in the rough here, kid. With the right plan you can turn this old place into a showpiece. We need to check out the basement first, though."

"Nick, I really appreciate you taking so much time with me. I've learned so much over the past few months I even amaze myself. I couldn't do this without you," she said.

Nick took the end of her long braid and shook it, dislodging a large fuzzy spider from its length, which he prudently didn't mention. He didn't think she'd get hysterical, but he wasn't going to chance it. "Quit thanking me! You're my family now. How could I not help my little sister? Besides, I stand to gain from this partnership, too. These are the kind of projects I've thought about but never really had the time to do. We both stand to do very well on this, Billie."

They had reached the kitchen and the door that led down to the basement. She was about to fling open the door when Nick held out a cautioning hand. "Hold on. Cover up your head before we go down the stairs. Let me go first, because there's no telling what's down there."

Billie was heeding his words but she was

sniffing the stale air with a frown. "Man, it really reeks in here! Is that what serious mold and water damage smells like?"

"It can. Look, you stay right here. I'm going down first," he said in the authoritative voice she knew meant business.

It was fruitless to argue with him, so she stood back with her arms crossed for more warmth. Chicago winters were brutal and even now, in the middle of April, it was still cold. When Nick opened the basement door Billie fell back and covered her nose and mouth. The funk that raced out of the cellar was indescribable. Nick frowned and shook his head, covering his own mouth and nose before going down the stairs. He was back upstairs in less than a minute with a tense, angry look on his face. Without saying a word he guided Billie out of the house to his truck. Once she was seated he went around to the driver's side and pulled out his cell phone. He made a terse call to 911 and looked at Billie with a grim smile that held no amusement.

"We're gonna keep looking for a house to buy. There's a body in the basement."

"Ewww," Billie said. "That's horrible!" She whipped out her cell phone and punched the button to autodial a familiar number.

"Who are you calling?" Nick demanded.

"Dakota, of course. If I don't call her we'll both be in trouble and you know it. An investigative reporter needs to know this stuff before anybody else," she reminded him.

Nick was making a grotesque face. "You Phillips women are something else. How you can be so beautiful and look so ladylike and be so tough is beyond me. My gorgeous wife is going to come over here and start poking around in that filthy basement like it was a jewelry store, isn't she?"

Billie flashed him the smile that had earned her millions of dollars. Even with the smudge on her face and a long fuzzy spiderweb still attached to her hair, she was glorious. "Welcome to the family, Nick," she said with a grin. "Life is never, ever dull with us."

He leaned back in the driver's seat to wait for the police to arrive. "I can see that," he mumbled, and pulled his cap down over his green eyes.

By that evening there was no trace of the tomboyish person who'd accompanied Nick that morning. Billie was at her sister's house dressed to the nines to attend a formal open house with

Nick and Dakota. Nick had to express his admiration and astonishment at her transformation.

"I don't know how you pulled it off, but you sure do clean up good," he said as he gave her a kiss on the cheek. "If somebody saw you this morning they'd think you were a totally different person tonight."

The events of the morning didn't show at all in her current appearance. After the police arrived and took their statements, they had lingered at the scene to see if Dakota would show up, and sure enough, she'd arrived and charmed her way into the house. Nick had been both amazed and appalled that even after making a minute inspection of the grisly remains, his intrepid wife had been able to join them at one of the diners she loved and eat a full breakfast. Nick had sipped a cola while watching the two Phillips women chowing down like they didn't have a care in the world and remarked once again that they were in a class by themselves. They didn't seem to hear him because Billie was busy telling Dakota how there were towels and old rags crammed under the basement door in the house.

"Nick says it would have smelled a whole lot worse if they hadn't done that," she reported. "Can I have some of your grits?"

"Help yourself, but I want a piece of your turkey bacon. And he's right, it would have stunk all to be-damned if the killer hadn't tried to stop the airflow a little. Real nasty piece of work, that was." She noticed that Nick wasn't eating. "Aren't you hungry, honey?"

He shook his head. "Most people really don't like to eat after they find a dead body, baby."

Dakota didn't look embarrassed in the least. "You get used to it," she said with a shrug.

"Like I said, you two are something else," he said dryly.

And Billie was indeed looking like one in a million for the event they were attending. She had gone to her temporary home, which was the brownstone that Dakota owned and had sublet to Billie when she'd married Nick. After a quick shower and shampoo, she'd deep-conditioned her hair and let it air dry before finishing it with a blow-dryer and hot curlers to set a head full of curls that she finger-combed into a tumbling mass. Her makeup was artfully applied and subtle, but it made her features unforgettable. Instead of wearing a simple black dress, the go-to frock of most fashionistas, Billie was wearing a cerulean-blue dress in silk jersey that was de-

ceptively plain. It was an unassuming little frock with a modestly scooped neck, long sleeves and pleats across the bodice. From the front it looked almost girlish, but the back of the dress was bare to the waist. The blouson skirt ended above her knees and it had a band that drew the eye directly to her fabulous legs. She was wearing black Chanel peep-toe pumps and sheer silk hose. Her only jewelry was big, gold, hoop earrings and a wide, gold, bangle bracelet. Nick grinned at his new sister-in-law.

"You're gonna have the men eating out of your hand, little sister. I'm'a have to keep my eye on you or there's liable to be a riot," he told her with a fond note of teasing in his voice.

"I never really wanted anyone eating out of my hand," she returned with a grin. "It sounds kind of unsanitary to me. Besides, the main reason I'm going to this soiree is because I want to meet Jason Wainwright. Anyone who's done as much in real estate as he has is someone I want to get to know," she said. "He's been in every business publication I can think of and every article about the future of residential real estate, blah-de-blah-blah-blah. He's supposed to be the end-all and be-all of real-estate sales in Chicago and I want to

know his secrets." She sat on the sofa to stroke
her sister's cat, Cha-Cha. She was a big Somali
cat who preferred men, but showed affection to
the few women she liked. Luckily Billie was one
of those women.

"Whose secrets? Jason Wainwright's?" Dakota
had joined them in the living room at last and her
entrance was worth the wait, to judge by the
smitten look on her husband's face. She and Billie
looked a lot alike. They both had beautiful
caramel skin, thick black hair and strong, sculpted
features. Dakota was tall, but at six feet, Billie was
taller. And Dakota had a figure that Billie envied.
She always said that Dakota was built like a real
woman. She had an awe-inspiring bustline, a
small waist and womanly hips with big curvy
legs. Billie always felt kind of bony and boyish
around her big sister, but she knew better than to
complain because Dakota would fuss at her about
her self-esteem if she did. Besides, her long
slender frame had earned her big bucks as a top
model, so she would have been a real hypocrite
to whine about it. Still, with Dakota looking so
fabulous in a violet crepe dress with a halter neck
and a plunging neckline, it was hard not to glance
at her own small breasts with sheer dismay.

Dakota's dress was artfully draped in the front and the skirt swirled away from the empire waist and showed off her legs in her Manolo Blahnik pumps, a gift from Billie, who'd gotten them free after a runway show. Billie had to laugh at the way Nick was looking at his wife. They needed to be leaving the house right now or Nick would talk Dakota right back up the stairs to the bedroom and no one would see the couple for the rest of the weekend. She decided she had to break the spell or miss the chance to meet her real-estate idol.

"You two are just gorgeous. I love that dress, Dakota, and Nick, your tux is slammin'. Let's go so we can pay our respects and leave early," she said hurriedly.

Dakota knew better than that, however. "You want to meet Jason Wainwright, don't you? Just watch yourself around him—he's supposed to be a big player. Real big," she added as she inspected Billie's outfit. "You can ask Toni about him. She's going to be there tonight, so you can get the scoop from her." Toni was Dakota's close friend and just happened to be the lifestyle editor of the paper for which Dakota worked. She knew just about everyone in Chicago, but Billie didn't care.

"I'm a big girl," Billie said mildly. "I know how to handle myself with some ol' wannabe Casanova. Besides, I'm interested in him for strictly business reasons. He's not even my type," she said with a sniff.

Dakota made a comical face to keep from laughing. "You're right, you're absolutely right, you are good and grown. But from what I've heard, Mr. Wainwright is *any* woman's type. Very potent, from what I understand." She paused as her husband held out the arms of her evening coat.

Billie slipped into her own faux-fur coat that Nick held for her while Dakota continued talking.

"All I'm saying is that you're so gorgeous you're going to knock his eyes out of his head. You're the type he goes for, hot and sexy. Just don't be surprised when he puts the moves on you," Dakota said.

Billie made a sound of disagreement. "Stop being so overprotective! I'll bet you that Louis Vuitton bag you've been eyeballing that you are one hundred percent wrong about this," she told her sister. "Nick, you're my witness, okay? I say he's going to be strictly business, and if I'm wrong Dakota gets my bag, which I haven't even used yet."

Nick chuckled and shook his head. "You're on your own, little sister. My name is Bennett and I ain't in it," he said in his Georgia drawl. He went out the front door first so he could help them both across the threshold. Giving them each an arm to hold onto, he looked down at them with a smile. "But I'm on Dakota's side on this one. Watch yourself around this guy because he eats up pretty girls like candy. Or he tries to. Be careful. That's all we're saying."

Billie just shook her head. As much as she appreciated their caring advice, she was positive it was totally unnecessary.

Jason Wainwright was standing at the top of the suspended staircase, which was the centerpiece of the atrium in the lobby area. He had greeted so many guests and accepted so many kudos and good wishes that his throat was getting dry. He took a flute of champagne from the tray of a passing waiter and sipped it while he watched the throng of fashionably clad partygoers on the main floor. He hated to admit it, but he was getting a little bored with his own party. He was hosting this gala event to show off his new office building on Lakeshore Drive and it was a smash-

ing success. His new building, all black marble and glass, was beautiful and the perfect place from which to conduct the real-estate business that had made him a millionaire several times over.

All the right people were there, the food was perfect, the music was perfect and the Moët was flowing. Even his date was perfect. Her name was Patrice and she was very pretty. She was an actress/model/singer or dancer; he couldn't keep up with all her aspirations. She had everything he required in a companion; she was gorgeous with a nice personality and no inhibitions. Since he never spent more than a month with any woman, he had no interest in the more intricate aspects of their personas. As long as she looked good on his arm, she could be flavor of the month and get his signature kiss-off gift, a Tiffany necklace. It was what it was and there was no use in trippin' over it.

He was deep in thought when his younger brother Todd joined him. The resemblance was there, but they were far from identical in appearance. Both were tall, although Jason, at six-four, was the taller of the two. They were both muscular, but Jason was slimmer than Todd. His cheekbones stood out in sharp relief and he had

a more sculpted appearance. They shared a deep-brown skin color, but Jason's eyes were the tawny color of sherry while Todd's were dark brown. Todd was clean-shaven and Jason wore a mustache and goatee with his close-cropped hair, a marked contrast to Todd's long locks. What they shared more than anything was the ability to read each other's thoughts. It bordered on clairvoyance and it excluded everyone else in their family. It was like a connection between the two brothers. At the moment Jason wouldn't have minded severing that connection.

"You look like you're at a funeral, Slappy," Todd said, using the childhood nickname that they often called each other. "You got all of Chicago to turn out on the coldest night of the year and you look like you just lost your last million," he said with a wicked grin. He scanned the crowd to see what was causing his brother to look so disenchanted with his own party. When his eyes fell on Patrice, he understood everything.

"I gotcha. You're getting ready to bounce Patrice and it's bothering you," he said.

Jason drained the last of the champagne and looked around for a waiter to get rid of the flute. "You're half right, half-wit. It is about time for

Patrice and I to go our separate ways, but it's not bothering me, as you so eloquently put it. It's not bothering me at all," he said.

Todd raised an eyebrow. "That's what's got you so upset, Slappy. You're getting tired of tossing away perfectly nice women, but you don't know how to stop," he said wisely. "You have no reason to dump her, but you're gonna do it, anyway. You need help, bro."

Jason didn't even bother to roll his eyes at his brother. "Drop the psychobabble, would you? If I wanted to hear that crap I'd start watching talk shows. Talk about something you know for a change."

Todd didn't hear the edge in his voice because he was looking at some people who'd just arrived. "Isn't that Nick Hunter? Didn't you say he just got married? Dang, his wife is fine," he said reverently.

Jason glanced in Nick's direction and he had to agree. Nick was hard to miss, even in a crowd, because of his towering height. Tonight he was impossible to ignore because of the woman next to him. Todd was right, she was a beauty. He'd heard a lot about the prizewinning journalist Dakota Phillips and he was looking forward to

meeting her. But his eyes were drawn to the woman on Nick's other side. Her head was turned away from Jason, but even from a side view she was a treat for the eye. He was wondering if Nick had a sister he'd never mentioned when she turned so that she was full-face to the two men. A flash of recognition raced through Jason, and Todd took a deep breath.

"Man, that's *Wilhelmina!* You didn't tell me she was coming tonight! Damn, she looks even better in person than she does in pictures."

Jason tried to act nonchalant, but he had to agree with Todd. The woman was beyond fine and he'd seen her in magazines, on magazine covers, in commercials and in a couple of movies. Suddenly there was no place he wanted to be more than where he was right now. He gave Todd his usual cocky smile and said, "I'll see you later. There're some people I want to say hello to." And with no hesitation he went down the stairs to meet the fascinating new arrival.

Chapter 2

Billie looked around the gathering with a smile on her face. She wouldn't have admitted it to Dakota, but she was scanning the crowd for a glimpse of Jason Wainwright. She didn't see him, but she was pleasantly surprised to see some people she knew. A tap on her shoulder was accompanied by a deep, chastising male voice. "When did you get to town and when were you planning to call us?"

She whirled around and looked up into the face of one of her dear friends, Antoine Brown, a point guard for the Chicago Bulls. His wife,

Chloe, was a college classmate of Billie's and she had been close to the couple for years. Billie laughed at the mock-stern expression on his face and gave him a big hug.

"I've been here since December and I promise you I haven't been ignoring you on purpose! I've talked to Chloe a couple of times, as a matter of fact. You were on the road and I know she's been too busy to mention it. I've just been going a million miles an hour, is all. My sister got married and I've started a whole new career and I'll tell you all about it later," she said with a smile. "Where's Chloe?"

"She's sitting over there—" he pointed "—waiting for me to drag you over. She's got a surprise for you," he added.

After introducing Antoine to Nick and Dakota, Billie went with him to greet his wife. She was a petite, pretty woman whose pregnancy was just beginning to show. Billie gave her a tight hug while expressing her joy. "This really doesn't qualify as a surprise, you guys. I was expecting this," she told the beaming couple. "After the first baby I knew you couldn't wait too long. How is my goddaughter, anyway?"

She was deep in conversation with her friends until she was claimed by another old friend. This time it was Kareem Davis, a linebacker for the Chicago Bears. He didn't waste time chiding her in the way Antoine had, because he knew she was now living in Chicago. Still, he was pleased to see her, which he demonstrated by picking her up in a huge bear hug.

"You're looking extra-fine, girl. Seems like the Windy City agrees with you," he said once he'd put her down.

She smiled up at him. "I love it so far. I've been working with my brother-in-law to learn how to rehab houses and I'm learning more than I did in four years of college," she told him. "He's going to let me be a project manager once we find the right house."

Kareem nodded his approval. "You're at the right place tonight, then. Jason Wainwright is like the real-estate god of Chicago. Have you met him?"

"Not yet, but I'm hoping to," Billie answered.

"Well, come with me and let me introduce you," he said.

Billie's face lit up and she took the hand he offered her. "Let's go. He's the reason I came here tonight."

* * *

Jason was heading toward Billie like a guided missile when Patrice stepped in front of him. "I've been looking for you," she said in her low, modulated voice. "Where have you been?"

She was looking at him calmly, without a hint of recrimination in her voice or anger in her face. It was one of the things he liked about her, actually. Patrice had the demeanor of a well-trained geisha. She was virtually without emotion of any kind and if she ever desired more passion from him she never expressed it. In a way being with Patrice was like being with an android, a beautiful empty shell that would only do what she was programmed to do. He had to force himself to smile at her and pay attention to her words, because all he wanted to do was find Wilhelmina. There was something irresistible drawing him to her and he couldn't wait to find out what it was. He couldn't be rude to Patrice, however.

"I'm sorry I was gone so long. I was talking with some people. Are you enjoying yourself?"

She gave him her usual automatic smile that didn't express amusement or humor; it merely seemed like another programmed reaction. "It's a wonderful party, Jason, but I'm getting a little tired. I had an early call this morning," she said.

Jason looked at her solicitously. "If you're tired why don't you go home? I can have the limo take you now, if you like."

Her eyes, made larger with the clever application of individually applied false lashes, blinked. "If you're sure you don't mind, that would be nice. You're so thoughtful, Jason. Will you be coming by later?"

He took her hand and squeezed it gently, which was for him an overt public display of affection. "Sure, honey. If it's not too late I'll come by. You go get your coat and I'll have the limo in front in two minutes."

In minutes he was looking around for the elusive Wilhelmina again. His date was gone and there was nothing to prevent him from resuming his trajectory. He caught sight of her on Kareem's arm and he frowned slightly, although he wasn't aware of it. That was the third man he'd seen her talking to that night. He could certainly understand the attraction, because she was the most desirable woman in the building. He couldn't hate all the men who were salivating over her, but if he could he'd tell them that their efforts were futile. He was a man who'd gotten what he wanted out of life by learning to trust his instincts and go

after what he wanted, and what he wanted was the laughing woman in the spectacular blue dress.

Billie and Kareem had to work their way across the floor because they kept getting stopped by one person after another. She had caught a couple of glimpses of Jason Wainwright, but it didn't seem like they were ever going to meet. He was busy circulating, the way a good host should. She was chalking the near miss up to simple bad timing when she saw him talking to a stunning woman who looked like she had a claim on him. *Oh, he's got his lady with him,* she thought. *Well, why wouldn't he, at a big bash like this. I'll just have to meet him some other time when it'll be easier to talk business.* Once that decision was made, she was about to tell Kareem that she was going back to her sister and brother-in-law when the sound of a deep voice stopped her.

"Kareem, I've been trying to get an introduction to this beautiful lady all night. What does a brother have to do to meet her?" Jason said with a debonair smile.

Billie raised an eyebrow and hesitated a second before extending her hand for a shake. "All you have to do is say hello. I'm Billie Phillips." There

was an odd gleam in his eye that she couldn't quite interpret and she was waiting to see what he was going to say.

Jason brought her hand to his lips for a brief kiss and missed the look on Billie's face. "It's a pleasure to meet you, Wilhelmina. I'm surprised to see one of the most sought-after models in the world at my event. I'm honored," he said in a low, silky voice as his thumb stoked the back of her hand.

Billie's smile vanished. "I'm Billie," she said firmly. "Wilhelmina is the woman they pay to pose. I'm the real person." She waited for Jason's reaction. Some people got it right away that she wasn't trying to trade on her publicity and that she wanted to live a normal life. Some people took a little bit longer to catch on and some never got it. She truly hoped that Jason Wainwright wasn't going to be one of those.

He was still holding her hand and she gently took it back, resisting the urge to wipe it on the back of her dress the way she normally did when someone glommed their mouth on it. This wasn't going as well as she'd hoped. He was a man who could give her all kinds of valuable insight into the world of real estate and she didn't want to write him off because he was proving to be as big

a player as Nick and Dakota had tried to warn her. *Okay, he's kinda stuck on himself but so what. I've worked with much worse,* she thought. It was true, a career in the fashion industry certainly equipped one to work with beautiful people who were overly vain, overly attentive and just plain lecherous. Billie had encountered plenty of men who behaved just like Jason Wainwright and it was no big deal. She knew how to extract the information she wanted while holding a pushy man at bay, so she wasn't worried. Besides, he had a woman. Billie had seen him talking to her and it didn't look casual. Even the most dedicated hound in the world wouldn't just dump one lady and try to hit on another one. At least that was what she figured.

Keeping a pleasant expression on her face, she tried to engage him in useful conversation. "I'm not modeling anymore, Mr. Wainwright. I work with my brother-in-law, Nick Hunter. Since I'm in construction now, I'd like to learn more about real estate, and if you can spare the time, I'd really appreciate an opportunity to talk with you about the market here in Chicago," she said. She thought she'd done a perfect job of expressing just what she wanted in a concise and profes-

sional manner, so when he pulled out a business card, she was pleased.

"If you're going to be in town, how about we have lunch tomorrow?" he asked.

"Well, I hadn't planned on leaving town anytime soon, so lunch would be very nice. What time looks good for you?" she asked.

Jason raised an eyebrow. "You're living in Chicago now?"

Billie nodded as she wrote her cell phone number on the back of his card. "I moved here in December. Here's my cell number. Why don't you call me tomorrow morning and tell me where you'd like to meet? I really appreciate your time, Mr. Wainwright. This is very kind of you. It was nice meeting you," she added. "I hate to meet and run, but I see my sister over there and she has that time-to-leave look on her face," she said. "I'm looking forward to tomorrow." She shook his hand again and turned to leave, completely missing the look on his face. If she'd seen it, she would have been much better prepared for the next day.

The ride back to Nick and Dakota's house was much livelier than the ride to the gala. It started when Dakota asked her about Jason.

"So you met Jason Wainwright," she said. "I

saw the two of you talking. What did you think of him?" She turned around in the front seat so she could look at her sister.

Billie shrugged. "He's okay. He comes across as being a little overconfident, but if I had his résumé, I would too, I guess. He's supposed to call me tomorrow for a working lunch." She looked at the lights of the city as the big car glided silently through the streets. "How well do you know him, Nick? What's your take on him?"

Nick glanced at her in the rearview mirror as he answered her questions. "I basically only know him through business. I know he's got a real good reputation for being honest and reliable. He seems to have real good instincts about the business. We're not like drinkin' buddies or anything, so like I said, I really don't know him. But I do know that he likes beautiful women and he has a big rep as a player, so watch yourself. I don't want to have to deal with him."

Billie knew that he meant every word he said, too. Nick was undoubtedly the most protective man she'd ever met outside of her brother and her father. She thought she'd better reassure Nick before he decided to make a preemptive strike of some kind against Jason Wainwright. "Look, this

is strictly business, Nick. I'm just trying to get the inside scoop on Chicago's residential real estate picture. I'm not trying to get with him and he already has a lady. But that's not an issue because I'm not looking for a man. He's nice-looking, but I know plenty of handsome guys. It's not like I just fell off a turnip truck. I can handle myself," she said.

It was Dakota's turn to look in the backseat at her sister. "*Nice-looking?* Were we looking at the same man? He's a little more than nice-looking, Billie. He's handsome, honey. Almost as handsome as my husband, but not quite," she said with a sultry laugh. "Nobody's that fine but my Nick."

"Ooh, you newlyweds need to quit," Billie groaned. "You forget I've worked with some of the best-looking creatures on the face of the earth and some of them were just that, creatures. Most of them were genuinely nice guys, but some of them, whoo-wee! Some of them were dumber than a box of rocks, honey. And some were stuck up and evil, too. Just because somebody looks good doesn't mean they have a good personality or morals," she said, yawning slightly. "Mr. Wainwright is handsome, I guess, but trust me, he

could look like a cartoon and I wouldn't care as long as he shares some knowledge with me."

They had reached the house and Nick told her to stay put while he warmed up her car. "I'm going to follow you home to make sure you get there okay." Billie leaned into the headrest and watched as Nick put his arm protectively around her sister and walked her to the door. It took him a few minutes to get back to the car because he was walking through the house to make sure it was secure before leaving Dakota, even for the short time it would take him to trail Billie home and return. She felt a tiny pang in the region of her heart as she wondered if she would ever have what Dakota had, a man who loved her beyond measure and would do anything for her, would protect her, would cherish her always.

Nick's hand on the door jarred her out of her daydream. "Come on, little sister, I got your whip warmed up so let's hit it. I don't like to leave my bride alone too long."

She smiled up at him as he helped her out of the car and led her to her own vehicle. They hugged briefly and she slid behind the wheel. The smile stayed on her face as she drove to her town house. There was something really nice

about having Nick worry about her, even for a few minutes. *One of these years I'm gonna have to think about getting one of those for my very own,* she thought. *But first, I'm getting a good night's sleep.*

Chapter 3

The next day, Billie rose early, as she always did, and as soon as she brushed her teeth she went in search of food. Breakfast was always the first thing on her mind when she woke up. The rumbling of her stomach usually woke her from a dream about food before the alarm clock went off. Today was no exception to that routine. After making an inspection of the refrigerator's contents, she assembled a bowl of granola with strawberries, a carton of yogurt, a slice of seven-grain bread, toasted, with peanut butter and a glass of pineapple juice. That was actually a light breakfast for Billie. She

worked hard and played hard and she liked food.
She didn't miss a meal if she could help it. While
she was drinking the pineapple juice, she looked
at her kitchen clock while contemplating making
another piece of toast.

"I'd better not," she said aloud. "I have too much
to do." She got up from the work island that
doubled as a breakfast bar and quickly washed the
few dishes she'd used. She swept the floor and
made sure everything was in place in the kitchen
before tackling the dining and living rooms. All she
really had to do in those rooms was dust, and she
could have actually skipped that step. Billie was a
very tidy person and preferred that everything
around her stay that way. This was partly because
it was her nature to crave order, and partly because
she was practical down to her bones. If she kept her
abode spotless it allowed for more spontaneity in
her life. She could entertain drop-in guests without
running frantically from room to room trying to
push things under beds and into closets, which was
the practice of some of her friends. And she was
too frugal to pay someone to clean up after her; that
was money she could put into her IRA or her investment fund or her savings. Billie had a plan for
her life and frivolous spending wasn't a part of it.

Once she was satisfied that the living and dining rooms were perfect, she went to the bedroom and changed the sheets before making the bed. After the bedroom was tidied to her satisfaction, it was time to think about her own beautification. She lay across the bed and thought about what she should wear for her lunch meeting. She turned onto her back and stared at the ceiling while she mentally assessed her wardrobe. "Hmm. Jason Wainwright is brilliant, educated and sophisticated," she said while she ticked off these points on her fingers. "He dresses like a million bucks." To underscore this point she turned over on her stomach and reached for the magazines that were stacked neatly on the bedside table. Each one had a story about Jason Wainwright and there were some very nice shots of him in business attire, as well as casual dress. "Business or casual? It's Saturday, so it should be not so dressy. But this is business, so it should be kinda upscale," she murmured.

She looked down at her long legs in her favorite plaid flannel pajama pants and then pulled out the hem of her pajama top, which was an old football jersey. "I've got to get some new

sleepwear," she said. "And I've got to get a dog or a cat or a bird or something. I obviously need someone to talk to because if I keep talking to myself someone is going to have me committed." She put the magazines back and went into the bathroom to shower. A nice hot shower with her favorite bath gel would get her head together and probably solve her wardrobe dilemma, too. Sure enough, once she bundled her hair into a shower cap and stood under the pulsing hot stream, she figured out what to wear.

After her shower she wrapped a thick bath sheet around her dripping-wet body and went back to the bedroom to slather her skin with body butter and lotion. She'd learned from her mother that putting moisturizer on damp skin helped it absorb better. Billie wasn't vain about most things, but keeping her skin smooth and moist was a must. Once that was done she picked up the remote control and turned on the flat-screen TV mounted on the wall. She smiled when she saw that one of her favorite shows was on and she danced along to the theme song as she put on underwear. "It's time to pimp my ride," she sang loudly, although she stopped when her cell phone rang.

"Hello?" she said breathlessly.

"Good morning. You sound bright and cheerful this morning."

Billie smiled widely when she heard Jason's voice. She sank onto the bed and focused all her attention on him. "I'm always cheerful in the morning," she said. "I have to confess to being one of those obnoxious people who wake up early in a good mood every day. How are you, Mr. Wainwright?"

The sound of his rich laughter had a strange effect on Billie. An odd tingle started somewhere in the vicinity of her navel and an equally foreign warmth radiated from the same place. His words lured her back to reality and she had to stifle a soft sigh as she listened to him.

"Wilhelmina, please call me Jason! When you say 'Mr. Wainwright' I think my father is in the room."

Billie raised an eyebrow. "Only if you call me Billie. That's what's on my birth certificate. Wilhelmina is the name I used for modeling and only people who don't know me call me that," she said in a pleasant voice that was none-theless firm.

"I apologize, Billie. I assumed, wrongly it seems, that Billie was a shortened version of the

other name," he said silkily. "I certainly meant no offense."

"None taken," she assured him. "It was something my agent made up to make me seem more exotic," she admitted.

Jason laughed again and the effect on Billie was even more intense. She shivered a little and looked around for her green terry-cloth robe. For some ridiculous reason talking to Jason in her sheer, scanty underwear made her feel exposed even though there was no possible way he could see her.

"How about lunch at one o'clock—does that work for you? I can pick you up and we can go from there."

Billie deftly issued a counter suggestion. "I'm going to be running errands all morning, so why don't I meet you at the restaurant?" He seemed to hesitate for a second, but he agreed to meet her. The name of the place he was taking her was Pax and he gave her excellent directions.

After they ended the call, she continued to sit on the bed to collect herself. Jason Wainwright had a remarkably potent voice. It had the same heady effect as a sip of brandy. She thought about their brief conversation at the party and wondered why she hadn't noticed how sexy he sounded last

night. *Too much background noise,* she thought. There was also music, noisy chatter and just too much going on. After talking to him today, though, she understood why Dakota and Nick felt compelled to caution her about Jason. It wasn't just his voice—he had some serious sex appeal happening.

Shaking off the feelings generated by the phone call, she stood up and went to the closet. There was no time for idle daydreams. She had to get dressed to impress and she finally knew just what she was going to wear: a pair of high-waisted black trousers with her favorite turtle-neck sweater, which was ivory cashmere and midriff length. She would wear her low-heeled lace-up boots and a short, black leather jacket for the perfect business casual look.

Billie arrived at the restaurant first and looked around with a little apprehension. Pax was light and airy with a minimalist lack of decor. Other than simple pale-oak tables and chairs and a few austere green plants, the place was devoid of decoration. There was soft music playing. Unfortunately it was the tinkling, quasi-classical, new age stuff that drove her

mad. There wasn't a hint of anything cooking
in the place, although there were a few people
scattered about the room who seemed to be
chewing. In Billie's opinion, a restaurant should
smell like food. The servers wore neat khaki
slacks and white tunics with mandarin collars
and they spoke in soft, soothing voices that
made her want to scream. *I just hope he's on
time,* she fretted. *If I have to be in this place too
long I'm liable to flip out.*

Her worry dissipated when Jason walked in. In
the broad light of day she could see him without
any interference and this time she understood what
Dakota had meant. As he greeted her and took his
seat across the table, Billie took a good hard look
at his smooth dark skin and his chiseled features.
It hit her that he was one of the best-looking men
she'd ever seen, and that was saying something,
considering all the pretty men she'd modeled with.
His tawny eyes were seductive and his lips were
beautifully shaped. They looked like they would
be the sweetest things in the world to kiss.

Heat surged into her face as she tried to squash
all inappropriate thoughts, but it was difficult.
He smelled clean and masculine and he was
dressed almost like she was. He had on a pair of

expensive-looking black jeans, an ivory crew-neck sweater and a black lambskin blazer. He also had on a pair of black leather boots that looked both costly and comfortable. He smiled at her again.

"You look beautiful," he said. "I think you're going to really enjoy this restaurant."

"It's pretty," she said as she looked around again. "What kind of food do they serve?"

"Raw."

Billie made a face before she could stop herself. "Raw? Like raw *meat?*"

Jason laughed gently at the horrified tone of her voice. "No, no, no. This is a vegan restaurant. They specialize in raw foods, totally organic and uncooked but prepared in a gourmet style," he explained.

"Oh," Billie said with a slightly deflated air. "So you're a vegan?" This time she tried to sound interested and neutral, but she didn't quite achieve that goal. The question hung in the air like a guillotine about to fall.

Jason laughed again. "No, I'm not. I follow a mostly vegetarian regime but I do eat fish and poultry."

A look of pure relief swept over Billie's face.

"So you're not morally opposed to eating chicken or fish or cheese or eggs and things like that?"

"Not at all," he said.

"Can we?" she asked eagerly.

"Can we what?"

"Go eat some cooked chicken?"

"Your wish is my command," he said with a slight bow in her direction.

Jason was still smiling at Billie an hour later as they finished their meal in a cozy bistro that served great soups and sandwiches. He'd had a cup of minestrone and half of a turkey sandwich while Billie had devoured a bowl of chili and a grilled ham and cheese. Her appetite was good and her table manners were impeccable, something he noticed right away. He'd had an opportunity to observe many women dining, and the number of them who lacked social graces was appalling. This was definitely a point in her favor, although she didn't need any more. He'd noticed other things about her, like her sense of humor and that she'd been direct enough to let him know she couldn't deal with the raw-food experience at Pax. The women he was accustomed to were so eager to be accommodating that they wouldn't

dream of demonstrating their own opinion about anything. They also shared a tendency toward eating very little, especially the models. He was used to being around women who picked at their food in tiny little bites. To see Billie really enjoying her meal was a new experience for him, new and very sexy.

Being with Billie was an unexpected pleasure. She was lovely to look at, of course, but so were all the women he dated. There was something else fueling the attraction he was feeling for her. It was beyond the sexual pull that was the norm at the beginning of a new conquest, although he was feeling the familiar primal stirring as he looked at her flawless, animated face. There was something unusual about Billie Phillips. She was obviously bright, as evidenced by her intelligent conversation. She asked a lot of questions about real estate and that alone set her apart. He couldn't remember a woman who'd prepared herself so well for a first date. Yes, Billie's essence was holding his interest. It was a unique experience for Jason, but he rather liked it. He had to force himself to pay more attention to the words that were coming out of her mouth than the juicy temptation of her lips.

"Have you done much work with rehabbed houses?" Billie asked.

Jason gave her an indulgent smile. "By rehabbed I assume you mean flipped houses? Not really." His smile turned condescending as he elaborated. "The real-estate business is getting flooded with naive amateurs who watch those little television shows about flipping houses and think they're going to get rich quick by buying a few old houses, fixing them up in a few weeks and selling them for a huge profit. It just doesn't happen like that in the real world and most of them end up losing their shirts."

Billie didn't reply at once, which gave Jason another opportunity to take in her fresh, natural beauty.

"I still can't believe you've stopped modeling. You have the kind of classic beauty that would've carried you for another twenty years in the business. Why in the world would you walk away from a great career like that?"

This time her response was immediate. "I modeled to make money to fund my future and my passion. Now I'm going to pursue my passion," she said with an intense flash in her eyes.

Jason leaned toward her over the table. He

propped his head in his hand and asked, "And what would that passion be?"

"Rehabbing houses," was her terse, dry reply.

Chapter 4

Billie couldn't remember a time when she was as happy to see a date end, even though her lunch with Jason technically wasn't a date. It was a business meeting, nothing more, but the result was a whole lot less satisfactory than she hoped. She was too honest to pretend she hadn't enjoyed most of it; Jason was attractive to the eye and quite charming—at least he was until the moment he revealed himself to be a pompous jackass. After that epoch-making moment the meeting had gone south rather quickly.

She had asked Jason to take her back to her car,

which was still parked at Pax. He had done so with a minimum of conversation, for which she was grateful because she wasn't in the mood for small talk. Now she was headed to Nick and Dakota's house and reliving every moment of the debacle as she maneuvered through the traffic. Jason the Jerk, as she now thought of him, had a lot of nerve, which was really too bad, because he was a darned nice guy when he wanted to be. He'd been great company with wonderful conversation and insight about her favorite topic, real estate. She could admit to herself that she was attracted to him in an unexpected way. How could she not be attracted to him? He was handsome, sexy and totally male—that was blatantly obvious. He was intelligent and he certainly had a good grasp of his business. He wasn't just blowing smoke. His success in real estate was deserved, from what she could see, and she found that quite admirable. But when he came out with his blanket condemnation of people who shared the same desire she did, she saw him in a very different, very unflattering light.

As soon as he uttered his withering opinion on house flippers, her assessment of him changed. Sure, there were people who went into the

business with dollar signs in their eyes and blinders on, but Billie wasn't one of those people. True, she was guilty of having an interest in home-improvement TV shows that bordered on fanaticism, but that wasn't why she wanted to go into rehabbing. Billie wasn't one of those people who thought she could gain sudden wealth by getting a house and taking it from a wreck to a palace in three weeks. Despite the many television shows that made it seem like rehabbing a house was quick and easy, she knew it wasn't. In fact, she hated the term "flipping" because it cheapened the whole process of restoring a home.

By now she was at the big brick home of her sister and brother-in-law. She pulled up behind Nick's truck in the long driveway and got out of her car, slamming the door with more force than was warranted. Nick was coming around the corner of the house from the backyard and he gave her a quizzical look.

"You look kinda pissed off. What's got your tail in a knot, little sister?"

Billie blew out a long, gusty breath. "Nick, do you think I'm a naive amateur?"

"Depends. You planning to play a round of

Texas Hold 'em with some professional gamblers, or are we talking about something else?"

Nick could always make her laugh. "No, I'm not talking about playing poker, although I can hold my own with a deck of cards, thank you. I just had lunch with Jason Wainwright and he thinks that people who get into remodeling houses are feckless, greedy dilettantes who end up losing everything."

Nick made an odd face, obviously trying not to smile at her heated anger. "Look, Billie, you can't take what he said personally. That's just his opinion, and to be truthful, there are some folks that get in over their heads and end up with a big mess on their hands. But that's not you. What have I told you about restoring a house?"

Billie pulled her right glove off with her teeth and began counting off the precepts that Nick had drilled into her head. "You have to make the right choices. You have to pick the right property and inspect it carefully so you don't get any expensive surprises like leaking pipes, water-damaged floors or mold. You have to pick the right contractor, someone you can rely on to get the job done right the first time. You have to pick the right real-estate agent to get the property priced right and get it shown right." She stopped

in her counting to give Nick an aggrieved look. "And when I get with the man who I think is the best broker in Chicago, he makes me feel like a total idiot," she said angrily.

"Then he's not the right agent for you, Billie. Pick somebody else, somebody who understands what you're trying to do and supports you. And can you do one other thing, too?" He looked down at her with utter seriousness in his eyes.

"What's that, Nick?"

"Go in the house. It's cold out here," he said, holding the storm door open so she could enter. She was laughing as she went up the few steps to the warm kitchen. The wonderful aroma of Dakota's spaghetti sauce filled the house and Billie felt better at once. Dakota was stirring the big pot of sauce and adjusting the seasonings. She greeted her sister with a smile.

"You look pretty, as always. How was your lunch with the real-estate mogul?"

"Just awful, thank you." Billie took off her jacket and hung it up in the hall closet before sitting in the kitchen with her sister. She quickly ran through the events of the afternoon and ended by saying that Jason Wainwright was

an obnoxious lout. To her surprise, Dakota
defended him.

"Now, Billie, don't be so hard on the man. He
doesn't know you so he doesn't know that this is
a lifelong passion of yours." She gave the pot a
final stir and put the lid back on before joining
Billie at the breakfast table. "I know it's something you've always wanted to do, but he doesn't
know that." Nick and Cha-Cha joined the two
women. Cha-Cha followed Nick everywhere, just
like a little dog. She doted on him, which amused
Dakota to no end because Nick had always
claimed to dislike cats until he met her. Armed
with a sharp knife and two big red apples, Nick
sat at the table with the cat sitting next to him,
watching his every move. He was cutting the
apples into precise, even pieces while he listened
to the discussion. Dakota directed her words to
him, as well.

"When Billie was little she used to look at
houses and figure out what she would do to them
if she lived there. She'd paint this one, put siding
on that one and add shutters, whatever. And she
worked with our uncle Roy every summer. He
was a master carpenter and she would follow him
around like his little apprentice. To be perfectly

honest, I wouldn't have expected her to do anything else with her life. Making old houses beautiful has always been her dream. You'll do great in this business, honey. You can't let one man's opinion get you down. And just because he shot his mouth off doesn't make him the enemy. He might turn out to be a great ally once you get to know him better."

Billie appropriated a couple of pieces of Nick's apple and frowned. "I doubt that seriously. Right now it's my fervent hope to never see him again in this life."

"Well, you don't have to if you don't want to," Dakota said mildly. "But you can help me with dinner, if you want. Toni's coming over and she says she has something to tell us."

Billie brightened at once. Toni was one of her favorite people and she always looked forward to seeing her. "I wonder what she has to tell us?" she mused.

She took another piece of Nick's apple and went to the sink to wash her hands while she chewed on it.

Dakota made a noncommittal sound. "Considering the last big announcement that Toni made was about that no-good sleazebag ex-fiancé being

a married man with children, I can only hope this time she has good news," she said.

"Ain't that the truth," Billie agreed. "I still can't believe he thought he could get away with giving her a fake ring and setting up this fake engagement. If Toni wasn't such a strong woman she wouldn't have survived it. I'm just glad they hadn't formally announced the engagement."

"Yes, but they were about to! The date for the party was set and the invitations were about to be printed. I know it hurt Toni to her heart, but I'm so glad his little family came trooping over here from Albania before things got public. That would have been horrible. It was hard enough to keep Nick from giving Ivan a beat-down. He believes in protecting people he cares about, especially when they happen to be women. He wanted a piece of Ivan's behind, but I talked him out of it."

Billie laughed. "I'll bet I know how you did your talking, too. You two really can't keep your hands off each other, can you?"

"Nope. And when you meet the right man, neither will you. Stir the sauce, would you?"

The delicious fragrance of the sauce assailed her nostrils as Billie wondered for a second what it would feel like if Jason couldn't keep his hands

off her body. *Where did that come from?* she wondered as she dropped the spoon, splattered the sauce and burned her hand. *Serves me right. Let the player play and let me keep my mind on my business.*

Jason wasn't often caught by surprise, because a man in his position couldn't afford to be blind-sided. But on this day, he had two shocks laying in wait for him. His first surprise was the reaction he'd gotten from Billie when he made his thoughtless remark about people who thought they could make big bucks by restoring houses and reselling them. He'd had absolutely no idea that she was trying to get into that line of work but he certainly knew it now. Once he saw the look on her face he knew he'd put his foot in it. He'd issued a glib apology at once, an apology that she brushed off like a pesky gnat. Even now he could hear her slow, measured voice as she'd responded to his words.

"It's quite all right, you don't have to apolo-gize for having an opinion," she'd said coolly.

He had tried again to make amends. "I've offended you and that wasn't my intention at all. I was speaking from experience, Billie. I've had

numerous friends try to get rich by doing that very thing, and some of them ended up losing everything and having to declare bankruptcy. If you believe what you read and what you see on TV, it seems like the easiest thing in the world to do, but it's a lot of hard work," he'd told her.

His carefully chosen words and soothing tone of voice hadn't done the trick. If anything they seemed to have the same calming effect as pouring gasoline on an open flame. Her eyes had turned icy and her face was distinctly unfriendly. "Well, thank you for your excellent advice. If you don't mind, I'd like to go back to my car now. I have some things to attend to this afternoon. Thanks so much for the lunch and the lecture. I really appreciate your time."

And just like that the date was over. He had to give her props for maintaining her composure and for doing something totally unexpected. He could count on one hand the times he'd been caught off guard by a woman, but Billie was proving to be unique. There was a lot more to her than just a beautiful face and figure; this was a woman with bite and substance. What was really rattling his cage was his reaction to her. Instead of being turned off by her, his internal

thermostat was turned way up by her personality and her fire. He was looking forward to getting to know her better. But before he could devote himself to that endeavor, he had a small task to accomplish.

He turned his Hummer in the direction of Patrice's apartment building. He had a Tiffany necklace to deliver and he didn't want to draw out the process. Patrice was charming and sweet, but whatever slight intrigue she'd provided him was over. It was time to move on.

He parked the big SUV in the visitors' section of the parking lot and entered the front door of the building. He waved a greeting to the doorman and went to the elevator. As he rode up to Patrice's floor, he checked his appearance in the mirrored interior and put his hand in his blazer pocket to feel the sharp corners of the small, pale-blue box.

He hadn't bothered to call before he came over because it was part of their unspoken agreement. He was welcome at her home anytime. He rang the bell and waited for the door to open and in less than a minute Patrice was there. She was dressed in loungewear, a long, silky, yellow knit dress. She was also wearing her usual pleasant expression, which could mean that she was ecstatic or

just sleepy. She always looked the same, regardless of her mood.

"Hello, Jason. Please come in," she invited. "Can I get you something to drink?"

He returned her greeting with a brief, dry kiss on the cheek and took a seat in the living room. "No thanks, Patrice. I'm not going to be here long," he said.

Patrice walked to the other end of the long sofa on which he was sitting and sat, giving him an expectant look. "I see," she said. "Am I getting my pink slip today?"

Jason sat bolt upright and stared at her. "Excuse me?"

"I think I'm being let go," she said calmly. "It's time for me to collect my necklace."

When Jason didn't reply, she assured him she wasn't upset. "We knew this wasn't permanent and I had a really great time with you," she said politely.

Jason's normal parting speech wasn't necessary and it was actually a huge relief. At least he didn't have to worry about tears and recriminations. He told her how much he enjoyed her company and wished her the best. He gave her the familiar blue box, which she didn't even bother to open. She was walking him to the door when

he asked what she was going to do with her time now that they weren't going to see each other. He was surprised that he bothered to ask, even more surprised by her answer.

"I'm getting married," she replied in her usual silky voice.

Before he could react to that bombshell, the door opened and Brice Hampton, the owner of the limousine company he employed so often, walked in with a bottle of champagne and a picnic basket. He watched in amazement as Patrice's whole demeanor changed. She giggled like a schoolgirl and walked over to Brice with a beaming smile on her face. "Hi, sweetie. I just told Jason our news. I'm sure he's really happy for us," she added with a sly look at Jason.

"Absolutely. Congratulations, both of you," Jason said as he left the apartment. He'd been surprised by a woman again. Twice in one day—that was a record that would stand for a long time. He didn't bear any ill will toward anyone. It was kind of ironic when he thought about it. He'd obviously facilitated their meeting on all the times he couldn't be bothered to pick her up or drop her off and he'd called the limo; that was obviously when they'd gotten together. If the situation was

different he'd have been furious, but this just made it easier for him to get to know the captivating Miss Billie Phillips a lot better. They might have gotten off to a rocky start, but it was nothing he couldn't handle.

Billie spent the afternoon making an apple pie and setting the table for Dakota. She had just finished when the doorbell rang. Wiping her hands on a paper towel, she joined Dakota in the living room to greet Toni. Toni was a former plus-size model and she always looked fabulous, even in casual clothes like the jeans and cashmere sweater she was wearing. She was tall, curvy and blond with big green-blue eyes and a great sense of humor.

"There's no point in prolonging this, so I'm just going to tell you guys straight out. I'm getting married," she said bluntly.

Dakota's eyes grew huge and Billie's mouth fell open. Dakota looked at Billie, Billie looked at Dakota and both of them looked at Toni. Toni burst into laughter and said, "Well, this is a first. I've silenced the Phillips women with one sentence! Why don't we adjourn to the kitchen? I'm sure there's something I can help you with while Nick watches CNN," she said glibly.

They followed Toni to the kitchen with blank looks on their faces and waited until she had taken a seat at the breakfast table before the barrage of questions began. Toni held up her hand for silence. "Whoa, whoa, hold up," she protested. "Let me give you the short version and then you can jump in anywhere you like. How's that?"

Cha-Cha leaped onto Toni's lap and purred loudly, which made all the women laugh.

"The boss says yeah, so go for it. As long as you give up all the details," Dakota warned. "You can't just drop a bomb like that and act like it's an everyday thing."

"I promise to tell the truth, the whole truth, blah, blah, blah," Toni said with a smile. "Well, as we all know, the wretched Ivan, the Albanian jackass, proposed to me and gave me that fake-azz engagement ring while neglecting to tell me that he had a wife and kiddies back home. I found out when he moved them over here, which was a big nasty surprise," she said with a flash in her beautiful eyes. "Besides being humiliated and heartbroken, I've been as sick as the proverbial dog lately with the flu. And Zane, bless his heart, has been an absolute doll. He wouldn't let me crawl into a corner and be miserable, even though

that's what I wanted to do. You know what a pathetic hag I've been lately," she said with a delicate shudder.

"Zane's been wonderful to me, really wonderful. He was persistent as hell, calling me and sending me flowers and bringing me food, but he was doing it to make me feel better, which it did. Until I realized that I had a really severe strain of flu. The kind it takes nine months to cure," she said dryly.

Billie's chin was propped in her hand and her elbow slipped off the table. She almost fell off her chair as she realized the full import of what Toni was saying. It hit Dakota at the same time and she covered her mouth to keep from squealing.

Toni laughed at their expressions. "Yep, that's about the way I felt, too. Only someone as under-handed as Ivan could have such sneaky sperm. You know I'm the condom queen and there was never a time when I wasn't fully insulated, because I wasn't aiming for single motherhood or cooties." She stopped for a moment and tilted her head to the ceiling while she thought. "Well, maybe it was just the incurable cooties I was concerned about. Being a single mother wouldn't be so bad."

Dakota finally found her voice. "But you said

you're getting married! Why are you getting married? Did Ivan get a divorce or something?"

Toni rolled her eyes and raised the corner of her lip in a snarl. "Ivan! Girl, are you crazy? I wouldn't have his head on a silver platter," she said disdainfully.

Now it was Billie's turn to regain her ability to speak. "So who are you marrying?"

Toni's cheeks turned a pretty shade of pink and she smiled bashfully. "Zane," she said quietly.

Chapter 5

Monday morning dawned drab, gray and cold, typical beginning-of-spring weather for the Midwest. Billie didn't really care about the chilling rain and the overcast skies; she was too caught up in her work. She had been hired to replace Nick's previous office manager, but since she was moving rapidly into a project-manager position, she'd started training someone to fill the office-manager position permanently. Billie had hired her a few weeks earlier and she was working out fine. Her name was Ayanna and she was a pretty, soft-spoken young woman. She

seemed a little shy, but Billie was sure she'd get over that after she got used to the office. She liked Ayanna a lot and tried to build her confidence every chance she got. She was showing her a new computer program when the office door opened and a delivery man walked in with a huge bouquet of bright spring blossoms.

"Is there a Miss Phillips here?"

"That would be me," Billie answered. She took the flowers with a bemused look on her face. He was about to leave when Billie told him to wait. "Just a minute, let me get my purse."

The man smiled and shook his head. "Already taken care of, miss. Have a good day."

The flowers were beautiful and smelled of spring, but there was no card. Billie searched through the stems, looked inside the cellophane wrapping and still found nothing. "Hmm. That's weird," she murmured. "I wonder who these could be from?"

Ayanna took the bouquet from her hands. "I think there's something in the conference room I can put these in," she said helpfully. "They must be from one of your secret admirers," she added.

Billie laughed out loud. "I don't have any of

those. Maybe they were delivered to the wrong Billie Phillips."

The door opened again as she was speaking. Jason Wainwright strolled in like he owned the place. "I assure you they were delivered to the right party," he said smoothly. "In fact, I have proof." He reached into his pocket and, with a flourish, presented her with a small envelope. Ayanna left the room at once and Billie's hand went out automatically, and she took the envelope without saying a word. She stared at it like she thought it was going to explode or something equally unpleasant.

Jason seemed amused by her silence. "Don't you like gardenias?" he teased in his best Billy Dee Williams imitation.

Billie didn't appreciate his humor. She finally looked directly at him and was immediately sorry that she had. He looked way too good for a Monday morning. He was wearing a sleek leather topcoat over a very stylish charcoal-gray pin-striped suit with a pale-blue shirt and a paisley silk tie. His hypnotic eyes had a sultry gleam that started that strange reaction in her stomach again. He was by far the handsomest pompous jerk she'd ever met. She handed the card back to him.

"Thanks for the gesture, but I'm sure your girl-friend would appreciate them more than I do."

He raised an eyebrow. "What makes you think I have a woman in my life?" he asked mildly.

"My excellent vision," she replied. "I saw you with a very beautiful woman at your gala and it was perfectly obvious that you two were involved. It may seem a little provincial of me, but I don't play that."

"If that's your concern, it shouldn't be. Patrice and I are no longer seeing each other," he said in the same low, sexy voice.

"Just like that, huh? One minute you're seeing her and the next minute you're not? Is that how things work with you?" The tone of her voice and her expression indicated that she didn't believe him.

"Actually, it was completely mutual. She's getting married to someone else. She told me this weekend, right after I had lunch with you, as a matter of fact."

Billie hadn't moved from the desk where she was sitting. She crossed her arms on its mahogany surface and stared at him. "Why should I believe you?"

"Why should I lie to you?" he countered.

"I have no idea. I don't know anything about you except what I read in the financial pages," she said crisply. She brushed a thick strand of hair away from her face and experienced a flash of self-consciousness as she realized how casually she was dressed in contrast to Jason.

That she was dressed to go to a work site didn't seem to register with Jason, which was borne out by his next words.

"I realize that you don't know me and I know very little about you, which is why I want to take you out for lunch and begin to remedy our lack of knowledge."

"You what?"

The amused sparkle was back in Jason's eyes and he stepped closer to her desk, close enough that she could smell his light, clean fragrance. "I think we should just start this encounter all over again. How's that?" He cleared his throat and gave her a small bow. "Good morning, Billie. I was thinking about you and I wanted to brighten this dreary day for you. Did I succeed?"

Billie tried not to smile, but a small one lit up her face, anyway. "You're persistent, aren't you?"

"Absolutely."

Just then, Ayanna returned with the flowers,

which she had arranged in a large ceramic vase. As Ayanna placed them on the desk, Billie gave a real smile, warm and dazzling.

"Thanks so much for the flowers, Jason—they're very nice," she said. She was looking at them and really enjoying the look and fragrance of them, as well as the thoughtful gesture behind the gift. She was so entranced that she almost forgot Jason was in the room.

He was saying something in that damnably sexy voice of his and she didn't hear a word he said. Ayanna had to give her a poke in the arm to make her respond.

"I'm sorry, what did you say?" She felt like a goofy adolescent having to ask, but nothing had registered with her. He patiently repeated himself, giving her his dazzling, disturbing smile.

"I wanted to know if you were free for lunch and if you'd have it with me."

Billie had collected her wits by then and she turned him down. "Thanks for the invitation, but I already have plans for lunch." She was very happy to be able to say that honestly. She really did have plans, work-related plans that she wasn't inclined to change. But Jason was apparently not programmed to accept no as an answer.

"I'm sorry to hear that, but I think I'll enjoy having dinner with you much more. I'll pick you up at eight."

Before Billie could say a word, Ayanna said, "That's fine. She'll be ready. Here's her address. She'll see you tonight."

Jason took the slip of paper from Ayanna's fingers. "Thank you…I'm sorry, I didn't get your name."

"I'm Ayanna Porter, the new office manager," she told him, extending her hand.

"I'm Jason Wainwright. Nice to meet you," he said as he gave her hand a shake.

"Same here," Ayanna said cheerfully.

Jason looked at Billie and said he'd see her that night. "I'm looking forward to this evening," he said, and then left as suavely as he'd entered.

Billie looked at Ayanna like she was a total stranger. "What in the heck got into you? Why did you tell that man I'd have dinner with him, and why in the world did you give him my address?"

"I told him yes because you need to get out with someone who isn't some old college buddy or a play brother or whatever and because that Jason man is too fine to leave hanging," she replied in a more forceful voice than she normally

employed. "And I didn't give him your address. That way you don't have to let him know where you live until you're ready to. You can just leave work early and go home and get dressed, then come over to my place."

Billie was amazed. This was by far the longest speech she'd ever heard from Ayanna and it was also the spunkiest thing she'd ever witnessed in the young woman. "But suppose I don't want to have dinner with him? Did you ever think about that?" She buried her nose in the flowers and closed her eyes to enjoy the first smell of spring.

Ayanna clicked her tongue impatiently. "Why wouldn't you want to have a nice meal with a fine brother like that one? Do you just feel like cooking tonight? Or do you plan to have a Lean Cuisine in front of the tube while you watch the game? All righty, then," she said crisply. "Just make sure you look extra pretty tonight. You both deserve it."

Billie looked around Ayanna's neat brick house with fascination. She had allowed Ayanna's enthusiasm to infect her to the point where she decided to enjoy the prospect of having dinner with Jason the Not-Such-a-Jerk. She had indeed left work

early, showered and dressed and tried to look fabulous, but like she wasn't making an effort. Ayanna lived close to her and this was the first time she'd ever been to her place, and it was a delight to the eye. It was so clean and tidy it shone. The hardwood floors looked recently buffed and polished and the walls looked freshly painted. The furniture was covered in a bright, exotic print and there were colorful pillows on the sofa and love seat. There were eye-pleasing pictures on the wall, reproductions of Thomas Blackshear, Paul Goodnight, Cézanne and Matisse. There were also healthy green plants in the windows and the whole place was filled with love.

"This is a lovely home you've got, Ayanna. So homey and nice."

Ayanna looked pleased with Billie's comments. "I did all the work myself," she said shyly. "Well, me and the boys." Before Billie asked, Ayanna said, "Come on in, guys, she won't bite." Two tall teenagers came into the living room. They were handsome young men with close-cropped hair and bashful smiles. "These are my boys, Alex and Cameron. Say hello to Miss Phillips, guys."

They both said hello and Billie could see their

resemblance to Ayanna. All three had black hair and sparkling black eyes with long curly lashes, toasty-brown skin and dimpled smiles. "Is all your homework finished?" asked Ayanna.

When they said no, she sent them off to finish. "It was nice to meet you, Miss Phillips," they said in unison before disappearing into another part of the house.

Billie watched them depart and looked at Ayanna with surprise. "Still waters really run deep," she said. "For some reason I thought your kids were really young. Those are big, handsome young men," she said with admiration.

"They were my sister's pride and joy," Ayanna said sadly. "When she passed away I took them and they've been my joy ever since. By the way, you look gorgeous and you smell really sexy, too. Your man isn't going to know what hit him."

Billie was wearing an amethyst-colored cashmere tunic with a big cowl neck that slipped beguilingly off one shoulder. With it she wore a black wool crepe pencil skirt and black Chanel knee-high boots. Her hair was smoothly coiled into a French twist with tendrils caress-ing her face, and she had on her favorite gold hoop earrings and bangle bracelets. Her fra-

grance was called Pure Turquoise and she loved it because it was sexy and direct without being too forceful. And because she hated wearing the same scents she smelled everywhere. This one was unique and echoed her personality. She was satisfied with her appearance, but not with Ayanna's take on Jason.

"He is not my man," she reminded the young woman. "And I'm not trying to knock anybody down—I'm just trying to get a free meal," she said dryly. "By the way, you owe me for this. I still can't believe how smoothly you set me up. You're normally so sweet and mild-mannered and then you go all gangsta on me," she said, laughing and shaking her head. She jumped as the doorbell rang.

Ayanna grinned wickedly. "He's five minutes early. Good for him. I'm going to the bedroom, you go open the door. Don't forget to smile," she whispered, and scampered.

The momentary panic Billie was feeling faded when she opened the door and saw Jason standing on the porch like he'd been picking her up forever. "Come on in," she said, and held the door open for him. His answering smile had the same effect on her that it always did—it made her melt.

"You look fantastic," he said warmly. "And you smell incredible."

She smiled at him as she picked up her coat from the sofa. He took it from her and held it out so she could slip her arms into it with ease. "Thank you, Jason. And thank you for the compliments. You certainly know how to make a lady feel special," she murmured.

"Are you ready to go?"

"Yes. Where are we going?"

He put his forefinger under her chin and brought her face close to his. "Somewhere they serve cooked meat," he said.

This restaurant was very different from Pax or the little bistro from Saturday. This place was rich-looking but understated and elegant. They were seated in a cozy booth with a high back that afforded them welcome privacy. There was music, but it was lush, seductive jazz. The lighting was muted but not too dim and the dining room wasn't at all crowded, probably because it was the beginning of the week. Jason took in the vision of his dining companion and was reassured by what he saw. Billie looked both relaxed and gorgeous as they waited for their server to bring

their meals. He would have actually been perfectly content to watch her all night, but he knew without being told it would make her uneasy. Besides, why should he just look while he had the perfect opportunity to get to know her better? He decided to plunge ahead with the obvious.

"Tell me something, Billie. The house where I picked you up—you don't live there, do you?"

"No, I don't. It's Ayanna's house. She had the bright idea of having you meet me there in case you turned out to be nuts," she said. "How did you know it wasn't my place?"

"It didn't look like you or smell like you," he told her. "So she wanted to protect you from me. Do you feel you need protecting?"

"Not yet. You've been a perfect gentleman so far."

He grinned at her. "I try to be. I was certainly raised to have good manners, but I'm afraid I didn't demonstrate them on Saturday. I want to apologize again for speaking out of turn."

Billie took a sip of her wine before answering. "Jason, you weren't deliberately trying to be rude. You were just being honest. You don't have to apologize for having an opinion that's different from mine." She had to lower her head after she

said that because she was practically parroting everything Nick and Dakota had said to her, but he didn't have to know that.

Jason watched her closely while she was speaking. The way her skin glowed in the amber light was amazing. Her lips mesmerized him the way they had before, and once again he had a deep desire to taste their sweetness. He exerted masterly control and tried to hold a normal conversation. "Billie, I appreciate your saying that, but it doesn't make me feel like less of an idiot for putting my foot in my mouth. Suppose someone asked you if you'd heard of a certain football player and you said you couldn't stand the guy, that he's a bum and a lousy player and his feet stink. Then the person says, 'Oh really? He's my brother.' You can't tell me you wouldn't feel like a bona fide, class-A fool," he said.

Billie burst into musical laughter, a full-throated sound of honest amusement. It was the first time he'd ever made her laugh like that and he found it both rewarding and arousing.

"See? Just hearing about it is making you crack up, so don't tell me I shouldn't feel like a jerk," Jason said.

Billie had to dab the corners of her eyes with

her napkin. "Okay, if it makes you feel better, you can beat yourself up, but it's not necessary. We can just agree to disagree about it and move on— how about that?" Her eyes lit up as their server brought their entrées, roast chicken for him and a petite filet mignon for her.

He waited for her to take her first bite, and he had to swallow hard when he heard the little *purr* of enjoyment that came from her silken throat. "Jason, this is delicious! Thank you for bringing me here. It's a really nice place," she said appreciatively.

"You are most welcome. I'm looking forward to taking you to many more nice places in the near future," he said in a low, sexy voice that she didn't hear because their server chose that moment to refresh her glass of wine. It was okay, though. Just looking at her enjoying her meal was enough for now. There would be plenty of time for everything else, very soon.

Chapter 6

After their delicious meal and the short walk back to Jason's car, he turned to Billie with a serious look. "Well, Miss Phillips, am I trustworthy enough to take you home or are we going back to the decoy house?"

Billie had laughed so much at Jason's amusing stories that evening her sides hurt, but it didn't stop her from chuckling merrily at the phrase *decoy house*. "Look, I know it seems extreme, but women have to look out for each other. She was watching my back because I'm new in town and I don't really know you."

Jason raised an eyebrow. "Oh, yeah? So what would you have done if she hadn't volunteered her house?"

"I would have met you at the restaurant or at my sister's house. That's how we do things these days, because you can't be too careful," she reminded him. "And to answer your question, we have to go back to Ayanna's house because my car is there."

Jason started his Hummer and prepared to drive. "Then we'll go there and get your car and I'll follow you home. I hope you trust me enough to do that for you, because if you don't I'll get you a police escort. Either way you're not going to be driving around Chicago at night by yourself. I won't hear of it," he said sternly.

Billie stared at him with her mouth slightly open. "You sounded just like my brother-in-law just then. That's scary," she murmured.

"Don't git scurred," he drawled like a certain rapper from St. Louis. "I just want to take care of you."

Billie was truly glad it was dark because her cheeks were flaming hot and she was sure her face was bright red. His words rested in the close confines of the vehicle like a caress and it was a

little bit too stimulating for her. She was actually relieved when they got to her car, still safely parked in Ayanna's driveway. Jason wouldn't let her get out of the Hummer right away, though. He had to start the car and make sure it was warmed up before he would consider letting her drive away. When the car was sufficiently heated he walked her to the door and helped her in, making sure she fastened her seat belt. "Drive carefully. I'll be right behind you, but take your time and watch out for anybody driving crazy," he cautioned her.

"Yes, Daddy," she whispered as he walked back to the Hummer.

They arrived at her brick town house in about fifteen minutes and she pulled into her driveway with Jason close behind. Before she could get out, he was at her door, opening it for her. He held out his hand and she took it as naturally as though they'd been doing this for years. They walked to the back door in silence, and when he held out his hand for her key, she surrendered it without a qualm. Her daddy and her brother always did the same thing. Once they were inside he insisted on taking a look around to

make sure that all her windows and her front door were secured.

"Jason, that's very sweet of you, but you saw me disarm the security system. I doubt that anyone is in here, but thank you for thinking of it." She was taking off her boots as she talked so she wouldn't scuff the hardwood floors. She started taking off her coat and he helped her with it and she took it from his hands with a sweet smile. She hung it on the coatrack by the back door and asked him if he'd like something to drink.

"Cappuccino, tea, spring water or soda—I have a wide selection available."

"I think I'll take you up on that. I'll have whatever you're having."

"Then take off your coat and make yourself at home. Come on in the kitchen with me," she invited.

Jason looked around at the spacious room. The kitchen was warm and homey, but it had all the latest equipment, including a six-burner range in the custom-made work island in the center of the room. He commented on the pleasant atmosphere, but Billie waved away his praise.

"I can't take credit for it. This is all Dakota. This was her place before she married Nick. In fact, Nick did all the work in here. The floors, the cup-

boards, the shelving, the living- and dining-room floors, he did it all. My big sister moved here last spring and got married in December, and since Nick already had a huge house, she sublet this to me. I'm kind of a vagabond right now."

Jason took a seat at the work island. "How are you a vagabond? Where were you living before you moved here?"

Billie was in the refrigerator taking out the ingredients for hot chocolate. After making sure that Jason didn't have a chocolate allergy or an intolerance to lactose, she began making her sinfully rich-tasting chocolate concoction. As she worked, she explained her earlier statement. "I was living in New York before I moved here, but I was sharing a sublet with three other women. I lived in Paris for a while, same setup. I've also lived in London and Montreal. Always in a furnished flat with roommates, with no real ties and no furniture of my own. I have a few things in storage that I'm going to have shipped here, but not until I have a place of my own to put them," she said as she stirred the fragrant brew.

"So that's why I call myself a vagabond. I'm practically a hobo, living here and there without anything that resembles a real home. The traveling

was fun, don't get me wrong. Seeing all those countries, meeting people from all over the world—it was fun, it was educational and edifying, it was great," she admitted. She stopped to pour the cocoa into two tall, flowered mugs. "But it was also boring, lonely and superficial. Anything that emphasizes your appearance the way modeling does is ultimately detrimental to your psyche. It'll make you crazy if you let it get to you."

"It doesn't seem to have gotten to you. You appear to be exceptionally levelheaded and well-balanced," Jason told her.

"I was lucky," she said modestly. "I have the best parents in the world and they gave me a good upbringing with good basic values. My brother and sister weren't about to let me lose my mind over some dumb stuff, believe me. Plus, I was older than these kids are now. I had graduated from college before I started modeling. Some of the girls now are in their early teens when they hit the catwalk. It's crazy," she said sadly. "You want to go into the living room?"

Jason picked up the small tray she had prepared and followed her to the living room. They sat on the sofa with the tray on the coffee table. She watched him as he took a sip from one

of the steaming mugs. "Damn, that's good," Jason said. "I haven't had hot cocoa since I was a kid."

"You're kidding! I live on it all winter. I'd take it intravenously if I could. I make it fat-free because high cholesterol runs in my family, but I make it better than anyone," she said proudly. "If you're nice to me I might give you the recipe."

Jason put his cup down and turned to her with a seductive smile. "I can't say I want the recipe, but you do have something I can't do without," he said.

He sounded so serious that Billie put her mug on the tray and gave him her full attention. "What is it, Jason?"

He quickly cupped her face and moved in close. "I want this, Billie," he murmured just before he took her lips in a long, chocolate-flavored kiss.

Billie was stunned into stillness at first; she couldn't move a muscle. Then the sensual warmth of his lips on hers took over and she felt a sensation like nothing she'd ever experienced before. Her whole body tingled with a sizzling intensity and she moved closer to Jason. Her arms twined around his neck of their own volition as his hands moved down her willing frame and

anchored around her slender waist, pulling her closer to his muscular chest. She was way beyond thought at that point; she was putting everything she had into that first magical kiss. His lips teased hers and his tongue pleasured her until she was dizzy with desire. They finally pulled apart, slowly and reluctantly. Billie's black eyes were huge and dreamy as she looked into Jason's tawny ones, which were warm and full of golden sparks. She could feel her heart beating in every part of her body, a rapid pulsing that made her tremble in Jason's embrace. It was as though they were suspended in the moment and neither of them wanted to break the spell.

Billie was the first to give in. She traced his lips with her forefinger and made a soft "ooh" of surprise when he captured it in his mouth for a sweet, teasing kiss. He released her finger and began to say something that was lost as Billie kissed him again. She'd never initiated a kiss before, but she had to taste him again, to recapture the amazing experience. As soon as her lips touched his he took control, lifting her onto his lap and holding her tight while he continued the delicious feast of her mouth. They might have gone on kissing for a lifetime but the in-

cessant noise of Billie's phone called a halt to their activity.

Afterward Billie's face was in a state of permanent blush because she hadn't heard a thing. It was Jason who had to break it to her that the phone was ringing. "Sweetheart, I think someone's trying to get you," he said gently.

Billie's long lashes blinked several times and she finally heard Ayanna's voice through the speaker of her phone with its built-in answering device.

"If you're there you have thirty seconds to pick up before I call the cops. You know you were supposed to check in with me when you got home."

Billie made a mad grab for the handset on the table next to the sofa. "Hello? Hello? I'm here, Ayanna. I, um, we, ah, we were just having some hot chocolate," she mumbled. She felt her hair come tumbling down her back as the big tortoise-shell pin that had held her twist gave way. She also finally noticed that her tunic's cowl neck was completely off her shoulder. While she was trying to listen to Ayanna she struggled to get off Jason's lap, and she did so as gracefully as a flamingo on roller blades.

"Mm-hmm, yep, sure did. Okay, yep, will do. See you tomorrow, Ayanna," Billie managed

before depressing the End button and replacing the phone on its base. After two tries she had it back where it belonged. She didn't want to look at Jason because she knew she looked ridiculous. He didn't seem to notice because he stood behind her and put his hands on her shoulders.

"Don't do that," he whispered.

"Do what?" she murmured.

"Don't turn away from me. I need to see that pretty face," he said gently. He turned her to him. Cupping his hands around her face again, he kissed her forehead gently. "There she is, the most beautiful woman I've ever seen."

Billie smiled up at him. "If you say so."

"I absolutely do. You're nice and tall, too. You're about six feet, aren't you? I like that," he said with admiration. "It makes it easy for me to hold on to you. I can't wait to dance with you."

Any embarrassment she'd felt disappeared as he continued to talk to her. His words, interspersed with little kisses on her forehead and cheeks, made her concentrate on him and nothing else. But he seemed perceptive enough to realize that she was working on a sensory meltdown and he said it was time for him to leave.

"I don't want you to be falling asleep on the

job tomorrow. I don't know Nick too well, but he seems like he might be a tough guy to work for," he joked. "Come walk me to the door so you can get some sleep."

They walked to the kitchen with their hands tightly clasped. She held his coat up for him and he grinned while taking it from her hands. "I won't need it, baby. You got me warm enough. Make sure you put that security system on as soon as I walk out of here. I'll call you when I get home."

Billie punched in the alarm code at once and then leaned against the door with a goofy, dazed look on her face. This was the best date she'd ever had in her life, and suddenly she couldn't wait to tell Dakota all about it. Well, most of it. Some things were too private to be shared.

Chapter 7

The drive to Jason's downtown apartment was accomplished in complete silence. He'd turned off the car stereo because he'd had quite enough stimulation for one night. Billie Phillips had filled him to the brim with feelings he hadn't experienced in years. Maybe he'd never really felt anything like it before, he wasn't really sure. He lowered the windows in the Hummer to let some cold air in. The heat he and Billie had created was like an inferno in his pants and he was burning up. When he'd asked Billie out he'd expected what he normally got at the beginning of his usual

hookups. They were supposed to go out a couple
of times to size each other up and then the sex
would begin. They would be seen at all the important events, maybe a side trip to the islands or
some resort, perhaps a trip to the NBA All Star
game or the Superbowl, if the season was right.
Then he'd get bored and move on.

That was how it worked with him, that was
how it had always been, and he saw no reason for
his pattern to change. But it wouldn't work that
way with Billie, he could see that already. The
questions he had to ask himself were what would
he be getting into with Billie and could she handle
it. He parked in the underground parking struc-
ture of his building and took the elevator up to his
penthouse apartment. If it hadn't been so magnifi-
cently decorated, the glass aerie on the top of the
very high-rent building might have been a cliché,
but it suited Jason. Everything was in cool blues
and grays and the very high-tech, ultramodern
decor said that he was a major mogul, which was
just the message he wanted to send. He hung his
topcoat in the closet, shuffled through the mail his
housekeeper had left on the nickel-and-glass
console table in the foyer and wandered into the
kitchen to get a glass of mineral water. He could

still taste the sweetness of the cocoa-tinged kisses he'd shared with Billie.

He drained the water, put the glass in the sink and went to the bedroom where he took off his clothes, tossing his shirt into the hamper for the laundry and his underwear in the regular hamper. The suit he hung in the closet, although he could smell Billie's provocative fragrance lightly clinging to it. He took a brisk shower while he weighed the odds of getting out of a relationship with Billie without leaving some scars. She might be sensual to the point of being highly talented, but Jason was no fool and he knew a beginner from a pro. There was something sweet and innocent about Billie that couldn't be faked, and he ought to know, because he'd dated enough women to know when someone was trying to seem like a novice. It was the oldest trick in some women's repertoire, the fake shyness, the "I've never done this before" wide-eyed routine. Some women clung to the belief that feigned innocence would somehow ensure a man's undying love, a belief that Jason had never encouraged. In fact, he usually dropped those phonies in a heartbeat. He had no doubt whatsoever that Billie was the real deal, however. What the hell was he supposed

to do with an innocent woman who looked and kissed like she invented the art of making love?

He groaned loudly because thinking about her in the warm fragrance of his pulsing shower had brought his erection back with a vengeance. It was like a hungry beast looking for prey and there was none to be had in the shower stall. "Down, boy. You may as well get some sleep because that tenderoni is a dish you may never taste," he said with deep regret. He knew without being told that if he made love to Billie he wouldn't be able to let her go. And that was the problem. There was nothing in his emotional makeup that could make that scenario work. A permanent relationship wasn't in his nature. If he even attempted a long-term hookup someone would end up getting destroyed and it wouldn't be him. He turned the water to cold and braced his fists against the walls of the shower to tolerate the icy blast. "Serves you right, partner. I told you to chill," he growled.

He got out of the shower, wrapped himself in a blue velour towel that had been warming on a rack and went into the master bedroom. His bed was huge, covered in a navy, sand-washed silk duvet with six goose-down pillows at the head. He turned back the covers, slid his naked body

between the silk sheets and picked up the phone. His word was his bond and he'd told Billie he'd call to say good-night. It couldn't do any real harm and he wanted to hear her voice again for reasons he wasn't willing to examine too closely. He turned on the stereo and despite his steely resolve, he smiled when he heard her sexy voice say hello. It wouldn't hurt to chat for a few minutes, he reasoned. The fact that the sun was rising when they finally got off the phone was another matter altogether.

The next day Jason's mood wasn't in any way brightened by an early-morning visit from Todd. He came barging in while Jason was pounding away on his elliptical cross-trainer and watching CNN in the room he used as a home gym. He liked being able to exercise any time day or night and he liked to do it in the comfort of his own home. When Todd entered the exercise room with a carton of grapefruit juice in his hand, Jason frowned. "Please tell me you aren't drinking that out of the carton."

Todd grinned. "I can't tell you that because I don't lie to you, big brother. There's not that much in here, anyway. So what are you up to

besides burning up calories you can ill afford to spare? You actually need to gain about fifteen pounds, Slappy. This is a medical opinion, by the way. I'm speaking as a physician, not as your brother," he added.

"I like my physique just the way it is, thanks." Jason rubbed his taut, lean stomach with its eight-pack of hard muscle.

Todd raised an eyebrow. "But how does the beautiful Wilhelmina like it? I saw you talking to her at the open house," he said, leering.

"Think twice, bro," Jason said in a voice that held a lethal warning. "I did more than talk to her. We've been out a couple of times and she's a lot more than beautiful. She's very special, so watch your mouth."

His brother choked a little as the juice went down the wrong pipe. Todd wiped his mouth hastily with the back of his hand. "Let me get this straight. You managed to meet the fabulous Wilhelmina, you've been out with her and you think she's special." He looked at Jason as though they'd just been introduced. "This wouldn't have anything to do with Patrice going around saying she's getting married, would it?"

Jason chuckled as he finally slowed his move-

ments on the elliptical before turning it off and dismounting. He took off his athletic shoes and picked up a towel from his weight bench. "One thing has nothing to do with the other. But it just so happens that I introduced Patrice to the man she's going to marry, so she really owes me big-time."

Todd demanded details, which Jason supplied, ending by saying, "It worked out real well for both of us. I didn't have an ugly scene to deal with and she got the man of her dreams. Case closed."

Todd's laughter filled the room. "So that's how you're gonna handle your business from now on? Just do me a favor, bro. When you get tired of that fine Wilhelmina introduce her to me, why don't you?"

The words were barely out of his mouth when an object flew past his head, missing him by less than an inch. Jason had hurled one of his discarded shoes and was about to launch the mate. His eyes were dark with anger and his voice was low and furious. "If you even *think* anything like that about her you'll be your own patient. Don't think you can disrespect Billie because you happen to be related to me. I'll maim you, boy."

Blank confusion was all over Todd's face. "Who the hell is Billie?"

"Billie Phillips is Wilhelmina's real name, the name by which she prefers to be called. Don't change the subject, Slappy. I could've put your eye out if I wanted to. And if you try me you'll find out just how serious I am. I'm going to take a shower. Be gone when I get done," he said, and left the room without looking back.

Todd wasn't offended in the least by Jason's behavior. On the contrary, he was delighted. He'd just had irrefutable proof that something no one ever thought would occur had happened. Jason was falling in love, and Todd was positive that he didn't know it yet. Suddenly life in Chicago had just gotten a whole lot more interesting, and Todd was glad he'd have a ringside seat for the action.

"Man, this is gonna be gooder than grits," he gloated as he let himself out of the penthouse. He couldn't wait to see what was going to happen next.

Jason wasn't the only one whose feelings were revealed. After a long talk with Billie about her date with Jason, Dakota was aware that her younger sister was totally smitten. The next morning she was still thinking about the way Billie had gone on and on about Jason. She and Toni were having

breakfast in their favorite coffee shop and she told Toni her reservations about the situation.

"I just don't want her to get hurt, Toni. Billie really hasn't dated that much, believe it or not. She knows a ton of men and they fall over at her feet, but she never really seems to notice. She has a lot of pals, but she's never had a grand passion and if this guy turns out to be a louse it'll break her heart. She was never a party girl when she was modeling. She stayed away from the club scene and the parties. I mean, think about it—did you ever see her in the gossip rags or on one of those Internet *blog* things?"

Toni was staring at her plate with distaste. The poached egg on toast was staring back at her like a big evil eye and she pushed it aside. "I refuse to admit reading any of those heinous Internet things," Toni said firmly. "Billie is a smart girl, which is why she stayed out of the tabloids. When they hit the catwalk some of the young girls get to partying so hard they lose their minds. Sex, drugs…and the men, honey, you wouldn't believe what some of them are into! Every year the models start coming out younger and younger and it's so hard for them to resist the temptation of the glitz and glitter, the fancy nightclubs and

the long weekends with so called celebrities. I've seen a lot of lives get ruined," she said sadly.

"That's why I wouldn't worry about Billie if I were you. She's too levelheaded to get caught up with a weasel. I'll be happy to dig up whatever I can on Jason Wainwright, but I think he's harmless. I can't think of any scandal that he's been involved in and you know I'm the queen of gossip," Toni said with a wry smile. "Although I don't know if you should trust me to investigate because I'm apparently not too good at it. I let Ivan Bashira make a big fool out of me, didn't I?"

Dakota frowned the way she always did at the mention of the name of Toni's ex-fiancé. "Honey, you can't blame yourself for that business. How were you supposed to know the man had a wife and children in Albania? He didn't even have the decency to tell you himself—you had to find out from the evening news," she said angrily. "It was awful and I know you felt humiliated, but it's all over and done with and you can get on with your life."

Toni stared at her glass of milk for a moment before meeting Dakota's eyes. "Yes, I can. I have two lives to get on with, mine and my baby's. Well, three, counting Zane's. One monkey don't

stop my show and that includes a big hairy hockey player who shall never be named again," she said cheerfully as she held up her glass for a toast.

They clinked their glasses lightly as Dakota laughed at her friend. Dakota had to ask her one question, though.

"Toni, I know you told us that Zane asked you to marry him because he knows how hard it is to be a single mom and he wanted to protect you from that, but how is this whole thing supposed to work? What's going to happen after you say, 'I do'?"

"What do you mean, what's going to happen?" Toni's face flushed pink. "We'll, ah, get married and after the baby comes we'll, um, get a quiet divorce," she mumbled.

Dakota was about to say something else when Toni's cell phone went off and she picked it up hastily. "Hello? Oh, Zane," she said with a guilty look at Dakota. "We were just talking about you."

Dakota discreetly went to the ladies' room while she thought that Toni had no idea of how complicated her life was about to become. Toni might not realize it yet, but Zane had some strong feelings for her that he hadn't revealed, that much was obvious. *Well, they're smart people. I'm sure they'll figure it all out soon.*

Chapter 8

Billie was blissfully unaware of her sister's concerns. She was sitting behind her desk at the office of Hunter Construction with a huge smile on her face, put there by the flowers that had just been delivered. Two dozen peach-colored tulips in a round vase were sitting on the desk and she was looking at them with dreamy eyes. Ayanna was impressed.

"Look at you! This is only your second date and you've already gotten two bouquets. You're going to have to get a bigger desk," she teased.

Billie shook her head. "I'm taking these

beauties home with me tonight. I love tulips and these are too pretty to leave here. He's really thoughtful, isn't he?"

Ayanna smiled. "I'd say so. I think he really likes you."

"I don't know about all that," Billie demurred. "He's persistent, that's for sure."

Ayanna put her hand on her hip. "Is that all you can say about him? Is he boring or something?"

"No, not at all. He's a good conversationalist, he's smart and funny, and he smells better than any man I've ever met in my life," Billie said. Her eyes turned dreamy as she thought, *And he's a great kisser, too.*

"Bonus, definitely," Ayanna agreed. "I do like a man who knows how to wear a good scent. And he's very handsome, too. We can't forget that. Hey, does he have a brother? How about an uncle, a cousin or any good-looking friends?" she asked with a smile.

Billie grinned. "As a matter of fact, he does have a brother. He's younger than Jason and he's a doctor. A *single* doctor," she said with enthusiasm. "Want me to introduce you?"

"No!" Ayanna's face turned red and she looked positively panicked. "I was playing, Billie. I was just kidding around," she said hastily.

Billie's cell phone rang and she picked it up eagerly, looking at the caller ID. She answered with a happy lilt to her voice. "Good morning, Jason. How are you?" Ayanna suddenly found something to do in another part of the office so Billie could have a private conversation.

"I'm just fine, Billie. How's your day so far?"

"Perfect, although I have to confess, I've had about three cups of coffee to stay awake," she admitted. "Did we really talk all night long?"

Jason's deep laugh caressed her ears. "Yes, we did. I can't actually recall ever doing that before."

"Oh, I'll bet you did," Billie teased him. "You were probably the best-looking boy in school and all the girls wanted to get with you. Your poor mother had strange girls calling her house day and night, and you and your girlfriend had the phone tied up for hours," she said cheerfully.

He didn't have a quick comeback for her remark; instead, he changed the subject entirely. "Listen, I have to go out of town tonight and I'll be gone the rest of the week. Are you free for lunch?"

Her expression of regret was genuine. "I'm sorry, but I have a meeting and two appointments afterward. Maybe when you get back we can get together," she offered.

"Of course," he said smoothly. "I'll call you."

Billie stared at the receiver after she ended the call. The words "I'll call you" from a man meant that you were never going to hear from him again. That was Man 101, the most basic class in the curriculum of modern dating. If Dakota had taught her nothing else about men, she knew those words meant "It was fun but I gotta run." She shrugged and began to get ready for her meeting. She was a busy woman and she didn't have time for games. If that was what Jason Wainwright was interested in he could keep looking because she wasn't the one.

Jason removed his Bluetooth earpiece and tossed it on the passenger seat of his Hummer. This was the second time Billie was too busy for him and he didn't like to admit it to himself, but he was a little annoyed. Jason was used to women who cleared their schedules for him at a moment's notice. Billie Phillips was an exception and he wasn't sure how he felt about it. Ever since he got his MBA and started making obscene amounts of money, he couldn't remember any woman refusing him anything. As a matter of fact, he was used to them queuing up to get next to him.

It hadn't always been that way. When he was growing up he was a big kid with the cruel nickname of Porky, and he was used to getting turned down—a lot. Unless it was some big social event that everyone was dying to go to, he spent all of his high-school and college years pretty much dateless. But when there was a big concert or cotillion or some celebrity-filled benefit, he had his pick of dates. Suddenly all the prettiest girls wanted to be on his arm, if only for the night. His parents had plenty of money and a hundred-foot yacht, and he was always on the guest list for every social event in town.

Everything changed when he got his weight under control. When his current lean-and-muscular physique made its appearance, along with all the money in his bank accounts, women started falling all over him and he was happy to catch them. He had a strict catch-and-release policy, however. He was never involved long enough to get serious because he knew what they were after. It was a variation on his younger years; they wanted to go where they could see and be seen, enjoy the luxuries he was able to provide and get their pictures in the society pages.

The big difference was that he was in charge

now. He decided who he took out, where he took them and how long they would enjoy his company. It was a system that had served him well for a number of years and he had no intention of altering his routine. It wasn't broken and he wasn't going to fix it. Or that was what he'd thought before he met the tempting Billie. There was something about her that was going to be hard to resist, but he was a man who liked to get what he wanted, when he wanted it. He wasn't sure if he wanted to change his game for anyone, including her.

Billie wasn't surprised that she didn't hear from Jason while he was out of town, but she was honest enough to admit she was disappointed. His behavior simply confirmed that he was a jerk. And she couldn't say that she hadn't been warned, because Dakota had taken pains to do just that. What really annoyed her was that she'd let him slip under her radar; she was attracted to him in a way she hadn't expected. "Well, screw that noise," she said aloud. "He's handsome and charming and smart, but it's not the end of the world, now is it? I've got plenty to do and I don't need to worry about Mr. Wainwright, do I?" she said.

This time, though, she wasn't talking to her-

self; she was talking to her new companion, Sadie. In anticipation of her upcoming birthday, Nick and Dakota had given her a dog. Dakota knew how much Billie loved animals and Nick wanted her to have some protection when she was driving around checking out prospective houses. Sadie was a big black dog that Nick had gotten from the Humane Society. She was just the right size for Billie because she couldn't abide what she referred to as "ankle biters," the little teensy dogs preferred by starlets and celebutantes. Nick assured her that Sadie was going to be a great protector once she got over being shy.

"She's a little scared of men right now because some jackass abused her. But what'll happen is she's gonna bond with you. And when she understands that you're her momma and you're not gonna let anybody hurt her, she'll be the best protection you ever saw. She'd take a bullet for you," he'd told her.

In the few days, the dog began coming out of her shell. She was already more relaxed and playful, but very well mannered. The vet thought she was about two years old and she was lovely. She was also housebroken and would go to the back door and make a polite

little bark when she wanted to go out. Billie was already in love with her. Sadic loved being brushed and going on long walks and riding in the car. She was still wary of men and would stand behind Billie whenever they encountered one on their walks.

They were out walking the Saturday after Jason went out of town. Billie had just finished venting about him to Sadie when they came back around the block to find his just-washed Hummer in front of the house. He was standing by the back door with his hand raised to knock. It was hard to say who was the more surprised, him or Billie. Sadie went behind Billie at once and leaned against her legs.

"What are you doing here, Jason?"

He gave her a long, appreciative look that matched his charming smile. "How about this—I was in the neighborhood and decided to stop by," he said.

Billie rolled her eyes as she urged Sadie up the driveway. "That line has never convinced anybody of anything. Try again. Come on, girl, he's not going to hurt you," she said soothingly to Sadie.

By now she'd reached the back door, opened it and disarmed the security system. "Come on in," she invited. "Now tell me why you're really here."

"I missed you," he said. "Who is this beauty and when did you get her?"

Billie led him into the living room, still holding Sadie's lead. She sat on the sofa, her hand stroking the dog over and over. "Her name is Sadie and she's a birthday present from my sister and brother-in-law. She was abused by an evil man, so she's a little unsure of herself around guys."

To her surprise, Jason squatted on his heels and spoke to Sadie in a soft voice. "Come here, girl. I like pretty girls like you. Come here, sweetheart."

Sadie looked at Jason for a long moment and then looked up at Billie. Billie unclasped her lead and Jason called her again. Sadie walked over to him slowly, but sniffed the hand he extended to her and gave it a tentative lick. Then it became a total love fest and Jason scratched behind her ears and stroked her silky coat.

Billie was amazed. "I'll be darned. Nick is the only man she's let touch her since I got her. I'm stunned."

"They know when someone really likes them. I love dogs and she could sense that. Now what's this about your birthday? Why didn't you tell me you were having a birthday?"

Billie stood to take off her jacket. "It's not a secret, Jason. Everyone has a birthday," she teased.

"You know what I mean. I'm sorry I missed it," he said as he rose to his full height, towering over her.

"You haven't missed it. Sadie was an early present because she was scheduled to be put to sleep, so Nick got her right away. My birthday is next week." She looked at the smile of relief on his face and brushed her hair away from her face. "Did I hear you wrong? Did you say you came by because you *missed* me?"

She started to walk past him to the kitchen to put her jacket on the hook by the back door when his hand on her arm stopped her.

"Yes, Billie, I did. I just came by this morning because I missed you and I couldn't wait to see you," he said. His tawny eyes caressed her with an intense warmth that startled her.

"I was just a call away, Jason. If you missed me so much why didn't you pick up the phone?"

He moved closer to her, his hand moving up and down her arm. "Because I'm not that bright. I'm also not accustomed to feeling deprived and adrift when I'm away from the lady I'm seeing."

Billie chose to ignore that, primarily because

of the tingling warmth that spread through her body as her eyes locked with his. "Do you go out of town a lot?" she asked softly.

"I do, unfortunately. I have offices in New York, D.C. and Atlanta. But I'm going to be cutting back on the travel. I have a lot of people working for me—they can hit the road for a change," he murmured.

They were so close now that Billie thought she could feel his heart beating. Maybe it was her own heart, accelerating as they moved to each other. Vainly she tried to keep the conversation going.

"Why are you going to stop going out of town?" she asked in a near whisper.

"Because of this," he answered just before his mouth covered hers in a kiss. She opened her mouth with a soft sigh to receive the gift of his warm, sweet lips and his talented tongue. She dropped her jacket on the floor and was about to wrap her arms around his neck when she became aware of a new sound. The kiss broke off as she realized that the sound was Sadie, growling at Jason. She growled again and pushed at him with her front paws, which were sizable. Billie was delighted.

"Sadie, you do want to protect me! Good *girl*," she praised.

"She almost ripped me to pieces and you're telling her *good girl?* Who's going to protect *me* from this marauding beast?" Jason demanded.

Billie laughed and kissed him again. "I'll watch out for you. She just has to get used to us touching in front of her and she'll know it's okay."

"Then I guess we'll have to do a lot of touching and kissing and all that other good stuff. Sounds like a plan to me. Let's get started right now," he suggested, and groaned when Billie stepped away from his embrace.

"No, let's let her get used to you. Have you eaten?" she asked over her shoulder as she and Sadie headed for the kitchen.

Jason went with them, telling her, "I had a protein shake for breakfast."

"Yum," Billie said with a grimace. "How about a cup of coffee and a piece of blueberry pie?"

She hung her jacket on its usual hook and Jason's followed it. He sat on one of the stools at the custom-made work island and crossed his arms. "Homemade pie? Did you make it?"

"Absolutely. Want some?"

"You have no idea how badly I want some," he answered. She was busy washing her hands and didn't see the look of pure desire that heated his

perfect features, or she might have taken back her invitation.

When she looked at him again, he was getting to know Sadie. He was admiring her shiny black coat, which was wavy and thick. She also had a thick ruff around her neck and upright ears. "What kind of dog is she? She's a good-looking lady."

"She's a litla," Billie said.

Jason looked puzzled. "She's a what?"

"A litla," Billie repeated. "A little of this and a little of that."

He looked at Sadie and said, "Your owner is nuts. I think you should know that."

Billie grinned. "She's part Lab, and I think she's part Belgian shepherd and she might have some rottweiler, too."

"Well, whatever she is, she's gorgeous. Even though her momma was a ho, she's a beautiful dog."

Billie threw a rubber glove at him and missed his head by a fraction of an inch. "Excuse you! I'm her momma and I'm a woman of infinite virtue, I'll have you know. Would you like some ice cream with your pie?"

"May as well. If I'm going to indulge I may as well go all the way," he said. *And as soon as possible I want to go all the way with you.*

Chapter 9

Whatever doubts Billie had about Jason were dispelled over the next few days. He more than made up for not calling her while he was away; they spoke every day now. Despite their equally committed work schedules, they also managed to have dinner twice that week. She also invited him to Nick and Dakota's house for dinner on her birthday and he gladly accepted. He also had a special birthday present for her. They were talking on the phone when he told her about it.

"If you can spare an hour or so tomorrow, I want to give it to you then," he said.

Billie was full of curiosity. "What is it?"

"Why do people always ask that? How can it be a surprise if I tell you what it is? You'll find out when you see it tomorrow. Can wc do lunch?"

"Absolutely. I'll even work a half day tomorrow so I don't have to run back to work. I can't wait to see it," she confessed, sounding as excited as a little girl. "Where shall I meet you?"

"I'll come by your office at twelve-thirty to pick you up, if that works for you.

He was there promptly, and after helping her into the car, he started driving away from the city into a residential area. Billie wasn't paying attention to where they were going; she was too happy to see him. He was wearing one of his custom-tailored suits, but it was softened by the silk, crew-neck sweater he was wearing in lieu of a dress shirt. She was about to compliment his appearance when he beat her to it.

"You look so good in colors. I'm glad you're not one of those women who think that black is the only fashionable color in the world," he said.

She had taken a little bit more time getting ready that day and she was wearing a short, fitted red jacket with black wool cuffed trousers. It was much dressier than anything she normally

wore to the office, but she was just feeling festive that morning. "Thanks, Jason. I was just about to tell you how handsome you're looking." She finally started paying attention to the neighborhood and asked where they were going. "It doesn't look like there are too many restaurants around here."

"You're right, there aren't. I'm going to feed you, but first I wanted you to see this. I think you might be interested in it," he said mysteriously. "And here we are."

They were in front of a brick bungalow that looked like it was bringing down the property value of the whole block. All the other houses were well cared for and pristine, but this one stood out like a sore thumb. The shrubbery was overgrown and ragged, there were broken windows and the storm door was hanging off its hinges, along with a few missing shutters. It was obviously vacant and had been for some time. The white trim of the house was peeling and the garage door was caved in. Jason looked at Billie expectantly. "Well, what do you think?"

"I think it's the worst house on the block and the neighbors probably hate it," she said. "I want it."

Jason took her gloved hand in his. "It's yours."

* * *

"What do you mean, it's mine?" Billie could barely breathe. She was looking from the house to Jason with wide eyes, not believing what she'd just heard.

"I mean that the house is for sale and you can get it for a very good price. You said that you and Nick were looking for a property for you to restore, and this one should be perfect. It has three bedrooms, a bath and a half, finished basement, fireplace and a lot of amenities. The previous owner passed away and his family lives out of state. They just want to get rid of it. There's not a lot wrong with it—it just needs updating. It might need some rewiring because it was built in the forties and it's going to need a lot more outlets and phone jacks, and it may need a new roof. But it might make a good starter project for you. What do you think?"

Billie's answer was to grab his lapels and pull him over to her side of the car for a big kiss. "I think it's wonderful! I think *you're* wonderful," she said. "Can we go inside?"

"Sure. I have the keys, so let's go."

As they entered the house Billie issued a running commentary. "That garage needs a new

door and the driveway needs to be resurfaced. This walkway needs to be redone. I'm thinking it would look good in brick with carriage lights on either side. That wrought-iron railing on the front porch needs to go and that metal awning does, too—it ages the house. It needs a roof to match the main roof or a new canvas awning—that might work," she murmured.

Now they were at the front door, which Billie was rubbing with the flat of her hand. "This needs to be sanded down and restained or replaced. It's all dried out and the paint is peeling. All this woodwork needs to be painted. I just hope it's not dry-rotted."

Jason opened the front door and Billie held her breath. She stepped across the threshold gingerly as she tried to take in as much as possible in her first view of the house. The foyer was medium-size with fussy wallpaper and a dated light fixture. The dining room was to the left and the living room to the right. There was a fireplace in the living room and big windows, which would make the room sunny and bright if it wasn't for the heavy green brocade draperies in both the rooms. The carpet in both rooms was also green, a medium-length shag

that was faded and unattractive, but it didn't smell of mildew or animal urine, which was a plus.

Billie wasn't really paying attention to the specifics of the decor. She was trying to size the place up for obvious signs of damage. There were no water stains on the wallpaper and no signs of leakage on the ceilings. She went down the hall to the kitchen. More wallpaper was in there and lots of small, inefficient heavily varnished cupboards, along with avocado-green appliances. There was also a half bath on this floor, a screened-in porch and a bonus room, which could be turned into a study or media room. Billie turned to Jason, her excitement clearly visible.

"Jason, this is incredible. I haven't even seen the upstairs and I'm sold. How much do they want for it? Nick will go through it with me, of course, but so far it looks like a pretty straightforward remodeling job. It just needs to be brought into the twenty-first century. I don't think anyone has done anything with the place since the seventies," she said. "How soon do you think I can get it?"

He smiled at her obvious delight. "As soon as you get financing. It shouldn't take more than thirty days to close."

Billie raised her eyebrows in surprise. "I'm not looking to finance it. I want property, not a mortgage. I'm paying cash. What are the comps in this area?"

Now it was Jason's turn to raise a brow. "Comps" was real-estate parlance for comparative sales prices. By knowing what similar houses in the neighborhood sold for, Billie would know what the house would sell for after renovation. To move a house quickly it had to be priced right for the market. Rehabbing was a numbers game; to make money you had to buy at a good price, set an ironclad budget that included all materials, labor, commissions and a cushion to cover any unexpected events. Then you had to turn over the property as quickly as possible because the longer you owned it, the lower your profit. The fact that Billie was familiar with things like comps wasn't a revelation to Jason; in their all-night telephone conversation he'd learned how astute she was. A beautiful woman with a quick mind and ambition was much more enticing than he'd ever imagined. He handed the keys to her.

"Let's go eat and we'll talk about the details. There's an agent in my office who can handle

all the paperwork for you. She's very efficient and thorough."

Billie took the keys and tilted her head back for another kiss. "This is the best, most wonderful gift anyone has ever given me in my entire life," she told him.

Jason stroked her cheek with his forefinger. "It's really not your birthday gift. I was teasing you when I said that. You're making the investment, Billie. It's not like I'm buying it for you."

"But you found it for me and that tells me that you believe in me and what I want to do. That's what makes it a gift," she explained. "You're a very special man, Jason."

And at that moment Jason felt wonderful. He'd never experienced a surge of that kind of feeling before and he wasn't sure how he was supposed to react. But with Billie looking so radiant with the happiness he'd given her, there was only one thing he could do and he did it thoroughly. He kissed her until the pleasure threatened to cause an explosion. He pulled away abruptly and claimed he could feel his stomach growling.

"I'm taking you to lunch before I try to eat you," he said in a mock-stern voice.

"I wouldn't mind," Billie said playfully. "Go ahead and see what happens."

The mental image that resulted from that innocent remark caused him to walk right into the door. He hadn't felt this horny and out of control since college, and for some reason he actually enjoyed the sensation. *I should be running like a thief in the night,* he thought, but when he looked into Billie's eyes he felt like he was coming home.

Nick was more than satisfied with the house. He and Billie had made up a checklist as a test to help determine if a house was worth the money and effort to restore it, and the house Jason had found for her passed it with flying colors. They made a thorough inspection from the attic to the basement and there was nothing that would require anything extensive, although they agreed that rewiring was in order.

"Back when this house was built there wasn't anything like the amount of electronic stuff that people have now, so we're going to need a lot more outlets and phone jacks," Nick said.

"I want to gut the kitchen and put in new counters and cabinets and make a half wall that will lead into the family room to make it look bigger and

brighter," Billie told him. "And I think we should add central air, because that's going to add more value. And what do you think about glassing in that porch to add more square footage?" she asked.

She and Nick were in the kitchen making notes on each room and the changes they planned on making. They would continue to crunch numbers when they got back to the office, but they were arriving at a preliminary figure. Nick agreed with her about the porch, because that would also add value, as well as taking it from a seasonal fixture to a room that could be used year-round.

"So I'm going to offer $125,000 for the place and I'm projecting a budget of $75,000, which would make the total investment $200,000. We should be able to get $300,000, which is a nice profit for eight weeks' work," Billie said thoughtfully.

Nick nodded his head. "Does that $75,000 include the broker's commission?"

"Yes, and a finder's fee for Jason, too. I want to keep business completely separate from the personal with him," Billie said. "If anyone else had located a property, they'd get a finder's fee, so there you have it." She looked around the cramped kitchen and was picturing how it would look in a few weeks with slate floors, granite

counters and stainless-steel appliances. Nick, however, was looking at her.

"Look, Billie, him finding the house was a business move, but it was motivated by something personal. Don't get it twisted," he cautioned her. "I think it's time we got to know Jason a little better. He's coming over for your party, isn't he?"

Maybe it was the inflection he put on the words or maybe it was just his deep voice, but Billie knew that Nick wasn't offering hospitality—he wanted a chance to size Jason up in person. She just hoped that Jason would still be speaking to her when Nick and Dakota got through grilling him.

Chapter 10

Billie was in a great mood, a festive, happy mood. It was her birthday at last and Jason was coming to her little party. It would just be Nick and Dakota and Toni and Zane, but that was more than enough festivity. Even Sadie was coming with them, both to get her used to being around more people and because Billie couldn't bear to leave her home alone. Besides, Cha-Cha had taken an improbable liking to the dog. Cha-Cha was a very eccentric cat and almost never behaved the way anyone expected her to.

It was just going to be a casual gathering, but

If you enjoyed this Kimani™ Romance novel, you'll love these
2 FREE BOOKS!

Plus 2 Free Gifts worth about $10!

Yes! Please send me 2 FREE books and 2 FREE gifts! I understand that I am under no obligation to purchase anything further as explained on the back of this page.

368 XDL ERS6   168 XDL ERSU

Please Print

FIRST NAME

LAST NAME

ADDRESS

APT.#   CITY

STATE/PROV.   ZIP/POSTAL CODE

Offer limited to one per household and not valid to current subscribers of Kimani Romance books. Books received may not be as shown.

Your Privacy — The Reader Service is committed to protecting your privacy. Our Privacy Policy is available online at www.eHarlequin.com or upon request from the Reader Service. From time to time we make our list of customers available to reputable third parties who may have a product or service of interest to you. If you would prefer for us not to share your name and address, please check here ☐.

The Reader Service—Here's how it works: Accepting your 2 free books and 2 free mystery gifts places you under no obligation to buy anything. You may keep the books and gifts and return the shipping statement marked "cancel". If you do not cancel, about a month later we'll send you 4 additional books and bill you just $4.69 each in the U.S. or $5.24 each in Canada, plus 25¢ shipping & handling per book and applicable taxes if any.* That's the complete price and—compared to cover prices of $5.99 each in the U.S. and $6.99 each in Canada—it's quite a bargain! You may cancel at any time, but if you choose to continue, every month we'll send you 4 more books, which you may either purchase at the discount price or return to us and cancel your subscription.

* Terms and prices subject to change without notice. Sales tax applicable in N.Y. Canadian residents will be charged applicable provincial taxes and GST. All orders subject to approval. Credit or debit balances in a customer's account(s) may be offset by any other outstanding balance owed by or to the customer. Please allow 4 to 6 weeks for delivery. Offer available while quantities last.

▼ If offer card is missing write to: The Reader Service, 3010 Walden Ave., P.O. Box 1867, Buffalo, NY 14240-1867 ▼

BUSINESS REPLY MAIL
FIRST-CLASS MAIL   PERMIT NO. 717   BUFFALO NY

POSTAGE WILL BE PAID BY ADDRESSEE

THE READER SERVICE
3010 WALDEN AVE
PO BOX 1867
BUFFALO NY 14240-9952

NO POSTAGE
NECESSARY
IF MAILED
IN THE
UNITED STATES

Dakota was making Billie's favorite meal and it was going to be a lot of fun. When Jason came to pick her up she saw that he was dressed in nice jeans and a gorgeous cashmere sweater that matched his eyes. They looked like the perfect couple, as she was wearing jeans and a sweater, too, but hers was a silvery-gray, chunky-knit angora and she was wearing big square silver earrings and an armful of silver bangles. "You look great," they said in unison, which made them both laugh. Sadie was still a little shy with him, but all he had to do was call to her and she came, after looking at Billie to see if it was okay.

She adjusted to her new seat in the back of Jason's Hummer very well. Billie was touched to see that Jason had put a nice soft fleece blanket on the seat for her. "Jason, that was so sweet. I'll take it in and wash it for you when you bring us home."

"Why do you need to wash it? That's hers. I'm going to leave it in here so she can ride with me anytime," he told her.

When they got to Nick and Dakota's house, Nick was at the back door and he came out to the car to get Sadie. "I don't want that wild cat of Dakota's running out the door when you come in," he explained. "You two go on in the front."

Sadie went with him and Jason parked the Hummer at the end of the driveway. They walked up the curved driveway to the front door, which was open. Billie was about to say something to Jason when a loud chorus of *"SURPRISE!"* stopped her dead.

She covered her mouth, and tears rushed to her eyes and overflowed as she realized that her father and mother were there. Nick's brother, Paul, was present with his wife, Patsy, along with Ayanna and everyone else from Hunter Construction. The only person missing was her brother, Johnny, who was traveling in Africa on business. She hugged her father tightly and did the same to her mother. In fact, she hugged everyone she saw. "You guys really got me this time," she said tearfully. "This was a total surprise. Dakota, you could have given me a clue, a hint or something that Mama and Daddy were coming to town," she said reproachfully.

"But that would have spoiled the surprise, sweetie." Lee, her mother, was laughing at her. Linking her arm through her daughter's, she gave her a coy look. "Now when are you going to introduce us to your young man?"

Billie felt a flush heat her face and she hastily made an introduction without trying to explain

that Jason wasn't her man. "Mama and Daddy, this is Jason Wainwright. Jason, this is my mother, Lee Phillips, and my father, Boyd Phillips."

While they were shaking hands and exchanging greetings, Nick came into the living room with Sadie on her lead. "I kept her in the kitchen so the noise wouldn't scare her. Cha-Cha's been grooming her and she's ready to meet her public," he said, handing her over to Billie.

"Daddy, come meet my baby," Billie said. "Isn't she beautiful? She's really shy, though, especially around men."

Boyd came over to his daughter and knelt down to get a good look at Sadie. She didn't back away from him; she sat calmly and sniffed his hands. But when she looked up and saw Jason, she stood and let out a little bark. Boyd looked from Sadie to Jason and back again. "It seems like she's not shy around *some* men. How long you been going with him and when were you going to tell us about him?"

Billie groaned and closed her eyes. This was not a conversation she wanted to have, especially with Jason so close by.

The party was a huge success. Billie had more fun than anyone, despite her father's ominous-

sounding question. Boyd had been teasing her, something he loved to do and something he did as often as possible. He would put on a stern face and start interrogating her about the most outrageous things, but she always knew when he was joking. He was only half joking tonight, though, and she knew she'd have to endure a lot of questions before her parents' visit was up.

Jason didn't seem to notice that anything was amiss, though. He'd given every appearance of having a good time, especially when Nick and Dakota revealed their new toy, a very high-end karaoke machine. Her family was very musical, especially her parents, and there was nothing Boyd loved more than getting a chance to sing. He sang, Lee sang, as did Dakota. Toni and Zane did a number, as well as Patsy, Nick's sister-in-law. Billie made a mock protest when Boyd insisted that she sing, but she gladly took her turn.

"Okay, I'm gonna sing, but I need some backup singers. Dakota, you and Toni come on and give a sistah some love," she urged.

The result was a rousing rendition of "It's in His Kiss" that had everyone clapping and cheering. Dakota always said that Billie had the best voice in the family, and it was true she had

a strong, rich contralto that was a surprise to anyone hearing it for the first time. All the singing and laughter made the party even more special. The house was full of good friends, good music and wonderful food, and Billie couldn't have been happier.

She and Jason were the last to leave and she did so with great reluctance, even though she knew she'd be seeing her folks the next day. She hugged them both and kissed them on both cheeks before letting them go. "Come over tomorrow morning for breakfast," she said. "You've seen the place before, but you haven't tasted my cooking in a long time."

"My doctor is very happy about that," Boyd said in his usual deadpan voice.

"Daddy, you are so wrong! You know I can cook," she protested.

"I know you *think* you can. That's what makes you dangerous."

"Many people have eaten my cooking and gone on to lead normal lives," she said haughtily. "Mama, you come over and I'll cook for you. I'll get Daddy a McBreakfast—how's that?"

Jason drove her home with his usual skill. Poor Sadie was worn out from the excitement and she went to sleep on the backseat almost at once.

"You've been holding out on me. I had no idea you could sing like that," Jason said.

"We all can," Billie said modestly. "You heard my mom and dad singing, so you know where we got it from. They aspired to be professional singers at one time, but life took them in a different direction." She smiled to herself and went on talking.

"When we were growing up, Daddy didn't believe in spoiling us. We had to earn extra money if we wanted something extra like concert tickets, the latest fancy sneakers, a special outfit or whatever. So we got to be entrepreneurs at an early age. We learned how to hustle, honey. He'd give us what he called seed money, but we had to pay him back out of our profits. So we used to have taco sales, chicken-dinner sales and we even had yard sales to recycle things we had outgrown and stuff we'd picked up from other people's yard sales," she said, yawning slightly.

"Wow, I'm really tired," she said more to herself than Jason. "Anyway, we also made money by singing at weddings, bar mitzvahs, retirement parties, anniversary parties…. Anytime somebody wanted a voice, we were there. One time this guy paid us three hundred bucks to serenade his lady after they'd had a fight! It

was so cute. We were standing under her bedroom window in the cold chirping away and she just melted!" Billie laughed heartily at the memory.

"It sounds like you had a lot of fun growing up," Jason commented. They had reached her house and Jason had helped her out of the car and was walking Sadie to the back door.

"We did," Billie said. "I couldn't have asked for better parents or a better childhood."

"It will probably make you a wonderful mother."

Billie looked at Jason in shock. *Where in the world did* that *come from?* she thought. He was taking off Sadie's lead and when he finished, Sadie went to the big fleece cushion that was her bed and lay down.

"I forgot to give you your present," he said.

"You already gave me a present," she reminded him. "My first solo project."

"In the strictest sense of the word that was a referral. This is a present." He took a small box out of his pocket and handed it to her.

Billie turned it over several times before opening it. It was wrapped in beautiful paper and underneath its wrapping was a distinctive blue Tiffany box. She opened it to find a gorgeous charm

bracelet with a single charm in the shape of a dog. "Jason, it's wonderful! I love it," she said happily.

"Then give me a nice juicy kiss and say good-night. You've got to get up and fix breakfast tomorrow, remember?"

"Yes, of course I do. Are you coming?"

"I have a couple of meetings tomorrow and I think your parents might enjoy some time with you alone," he said smoothly. "Now where's my kiss?"

Billie held out her wrist. "Put my bracelet on first, please."

While he accomplished that small task, Billie looked at his handsome face and could feel her heart starting the rapid beat that was becoming all too familiar when Jason was near. As soon as he finished fastening the clasp her arms were around his neck and she was kissing him shamelessly. Their mouths were busy devouring the sweetness of their kiss and their tongues were involved in long, arousing strokes that made both of them unaware of the phone until the answering machine clicked and her father's voice came booming into the kitchen.

"I trust that you're not answering this call because you're taking a bath or saying your prayers. I know that man is on his way to his

house, so I don't have to come and…" Mercifully, the recording ran out before he could continue.

"Just for that you need to stay, Jason. He and Nick are probably cruising my block right now, so let's give them something to see," Billie said mischievously.

"Not on your life. Your dad looks like he can handle a gun real well."

"He was a sharpshooter in the army. Does that count?"

Jason laughed at her deliberately innocent voice. "Yes, darlin', it sure does. I'm not taking any chances. I'll call you tomorrow. Maybe we can all go to dinner or a play or something," he suggested.

Billie kissed him again and locked the door after he left. While she was punching in the alarm code she found herself singing. She danced up the stairs with Sadie on her heels.

The next morning she was extremely pleased to be cooking breakfast for her parents. She needed something to keep her mind occupied, for one thing, and she needed her mother's counsel, for another. Billie and Dakota had a very open relationship with their parents and never hesitated to talk to their mother about anything

and everything that was on their minds. Today was no exception. She made a wonderful breakfast that suited even Boyd, who was happy to admit he'd been wrong.

"Check out my baby girl! Scrambled eggs, homemade biscuits, salmon patties and peach preserves. And you remembered the rice, too," he praised her after saying grace.

"Daddy, everyone knows you like rice with your salmon patties, instead of grits. How could I forget that?"

He didn't answer for a moment while he savored his food. "Delicious. Your mother taught you well, Billie. This is fit for a king." He ate with a good appetite and after having two cups of tea, which he preferred in the morning to coffee, he decided to take a walk around the neighborhood.

"I'm taking my grand-dog with me. Since you all won't give us any grandbabies I may as well adopt your pets," he said pointedly.

He and Sadie left the ladies laughing. The door had no sooner closed behind him when Dakota entered. "I know you made biscuits and I want one," she pleaded.

"Help yourself. How did you manage to drag

yourself away from your handsome husband?" Billie said, only half teasing.

"He took his beloved Escalade in to be detailed. Now why are you looking so blue? Doesn't she look sad, Mama?"

Lee agreed with her. "I was just getting ready to find out what's bothering her. I knew she was just waiting for her daddy to leave the room. What is it, sweetie?"

Billie had been wiping off the counters and tidying up the kitchen. She sighed and took a magazine off the top of the refrigerator before joining them at the table. "I was so keyed up after the party I didn't go right to sleep. I started reading this magazine and look what I found," she said angrily as she pointed to a picture in the section of the magazine devoted to celebrity chatter.

It was a picture taken at a charity event that had taken place the week before in New York. And the picture was of Jason sitting hugged up with some slinky little singer with fake boobs and a weave that probably cost as much as the gown she was wearing. Billie was not happy, not in the least.

"I knew he was going out of town, but he didn't call me one time while he was gone and now I know why. Everybody warned me that he was a

big-time player and I didn't listen. I could just kick myself!"

Lee was studying the picture carefully. She raised her eyes to Billie's and said, "Why? Why would you want to kick yourself just because he's sitting with some young girl at a charity affair?"

Billie was surprised at her mother's casual tone of voice. "Well, because I trusted him," she sputtered.

"And has he violated that trust? No," Lee answered her own question.

"Honey, I saw him with you last night and I see this picture, and believe me, he's not looking at that little miss the way he was looking at you. Matter of fact, he's not looking at her at all, he's just sitting there. She's the one pawing at him, not the other way around. Now when the man does something that requires you to be angry, I'll get mad with you. But I don't really think this qualifies, dear one. What do you think, Dakota?"

Dakota completed her own investigation of the picture and was shaking her head as she closed the magazine. "Mama's got it right, Billie. It's just a picture and it means nothing. I've seen you in pictures with everybody from Denzel to Diddy and I never assumed you were having an affair

with any of them." She reached over and patted her sister's hand. "If he does something that's really scandalous or low-down, you know we'll have your back. But this isn't it," she said. "I wouldn't worry about it if I were you."

Billie felt utterly relieved by their words. "You're right. I was overreacting. I'm glad we got that out in the open because he wants to take you and Daddy to dinner today."

Lee's eyes widened. "You were going to make your daddy miss out on a free meal? Girl, what were you thinking?" She laughed.

Billie joined the laughter with a light heart. She'd spent a sleepless night for nothing. Everything was going to be fine.

Chapter 11

Jason traveled often and being away from home never bothered him at all. The luxury hotels he used had the same ambiance as his penthouse, so he felt at home wherever he was. He didn't miss contact with his family because aside from Todd, he wasn't that close to them. He usually spoke to Todd every day even if they didn't see each other for a week or so. The only other daily calls he made were to the office where his highly efficient staff handled things in his absence. Any woman with whom he was involved learned very quickly that he wouldn't bother to call while he was away

because it wasn't his nature. But now as he lay across the king-size bed of his suite he found himself breaking yet another of his unwritten rules of behavior, and once again it was all due to the captivating Miss Billie Phillips. It was a week after her birthday and he'd seen her or talked to her every day since, another record for him.

He put his cell phone to his ear and said, "Billie." The voice activation did its job and he was listening to the phone ring, waiting to hear her sultry voice.

"Hello, Jason. How's Atlanta?"

He had to close his eyes as the sweet sound he'd wanted to hear washed over him. It was the damnedest sensation in the world; he was both aroused and relaxed at the same time. The really strange thing was that she wasn't doing anything but being herself. God help him if she decided to deliberately seduce him, because he'd probably pass out from sheer pleasure. As it was, all she had to do was say his name and his pulse rate increased. Pretty soon he'd be breathing hard and sweating, if he didn't get a grip.

"Hello, Billie. Atlanta is boring without you. Have you ever been here?"

"Lots of times. I love it there. It's one of my

favorite places." Her voice dropped to a lower, even sexier register. "And you are my favorite person. Jason, the house is perfect for me. I closed on it today and we're going to get started on it Monday. You're the most thoughtful man I've ever met. I can't tell you how much I appreciate your help."

He felt ridiculously pleased by her praise and her thanks, but he didn't want her feeling indebted to him and he told her so. "It was nothing, Billie. I have tons of listings that come through my office every day and I knew what you were looking for. How could I not put you on to a good buy?"

Billie sighed and the soft sound stroked his senses like the touch of her hand. He wanted to ask her not to do it again, but he didn't want to let her know how she was making him feel. And he also wanted her to do it again because he liked the ripple that it sent down his spine. He listened to her words carefully.

"Jason, it's not just about you hooking me up with the house, it's about you taking me seriously as a businessperson. That means a lot to me. It's like I told you the other night, outside of my family there are very few people who really know me, the

whole me. Other people just know bits and pieces of who I am. In high school I was Beanie, Dakota's stringbean sister. In college I was the super-jock basketball geek and then I was Wilhelmina, thanks to a pound of makeup and some really good lighting. Now I feel like the real Billie again and you're a part of that," she confessed.

Jason had to sit up after that innocent statement of trust and confidence. The only thing that could have kept him away from her after that was the couple of thousand miles between them. Now, what he'd do with her if they were in the same place right now… Her voice derailed the lust train that was about to leave his mental station. Her voice brought him back to earth.

"When are you coming home?"

"I'll be back on Friday. And I want to do something special with you, so don't make any plans, okay?"

As they ended the call he realized he'd just made a date for Friday night and it was only Tuesday. In his entire life he'd never done anything like that. Billie Phillips was a dangerous woman and he was just beginning to realize how much he liked playing with fire.

* * *

Billie had been waiting for this all week. It was Friday at last and Jason was coming home and they had a special date. He still hadn't given her any details, but that just added to her anticipation. They had talked every day while he was away. He called her every morning and every night and he refused to give her even one little hint about their date. He said that all would be revealed when he returned, so she had to be content with that. No matter what he selected for their rendezvous, she was going to be ready with her *A* game.

She'd gone in to work early so she could leave early to indulge in a few beauty treatments, something she almost never did. She could do her own manicures and pedicures and normally she did, but today she decided to treat herself to the works. A cleansing facial, a massage, a manicure, pedicure and a roller set for her hair took up her entire afternoon, but the results were worth it. Even to her own critical eye she looked fabulous.

Now all she had to do was figure out what to wear. Billie had a very specific wardrobe. She didn't have a huge closet spilling over with

designer clothing, because that just wasn't her style. She had six pairs of dress slacks and six pairs of jeans, four white dress shirts, two black ones and so forth. She didn't like having a ton of clothes that she wouldn't wear more than once or twice, so she kept things classic and to a minimum. She bought pieces that could be mixed and matched and worn with things she already had, and once she made a new purchase, something in her closet went to charity or to a friend. She knew models who had converted entire rooms in their homes to closets and she just didn't feel the need for all that. Clothes weren't that important to her. Underwear, yes, but clothing, not so much.

She was wearing a new set of her favorite designer underwear, a soft-pink half-cup bra in silk with embroidered leaves and flowers embellishing the cups and a matching bikini panty in the same design, but that was all she was wearing. Her phone rang and she left the closet to go answer it. It was Jason and the smile on her face could be heard in her greeting.

"Hello, Jason. Did you have a nice flight?"

"Hello, beautiful. Yes, I had a great trip, made my connection with no delays and I didn't get

strip-searched, so it was a good day," he said dryly. "How are you?"

"I'm dying of curiosity, that's how I am. I'm trying to get dressed and I have no idea what to wear," she chided him. "Can't you give me a hint?"

"Wear what you have on," he suggested. "This is going to be a very casual evening."

Billie laughed and said she didn't think what she had on would be appropriate. "I'm wearing LaPerla and nothing else," she said.

"I'm not as well-educated about women's clothing as you might think, but isn't that lingerie?"

"Yes, it is. But now that I know this is a casual affair I can add to my ensemble," she said cheerfully.

"Listen, doll, you can throw a coat on and come just as you are, I'm not fussy. Really I'm not," he assured her.

"And I'm not that bold. What are you wearing?" she asked.

"Just jeans and a shirt. Like I said, this is a real laid-back evening."

"So what time is this casual date taking place?"

"I'll come get you at eight, if that's okay."

"I'll be ready."

Now that she knew what the proper attire was,

she dressed quickly in her favorite jeans and a white shirt worn over a lacy pink camisole. She also put on her favorite flats, a pair of bronze leather ballet slippers. A little perfume and a little lip gloss and she was ready to go. Her makeup was minimal as always, just a bronzer brushed along her cheekbones and on her eyelids, and her favorite mascara. Her hair was gorgeous, shiny and full of waves from her roller set earlier. She was satisfied that she looked sufficiently relaxed but feminine, and it was a good thing, because her doorbell rang at five minutes to eight.

She had seen Jason in a variety of dress clothes, but he looked even sexier in a plain raw-silk shirt and a pair of jeans that emphasized the length of his legs. They hugged briefly and he gave her a sweet little kiss on the forehead. He also gave Sadie her customary head rub and ear scratch while he urged Billie to make haste.

"I don't mean to rush you, but we have reservations so we need to get going."

He helped Billie on with her coat and after she set the alarm system, he seated her in the Hummer before getting behind the wheel. In a short time they had arrived at a tall building on Lakeshore Drive and entered the underground

parking. As he escorted her to the building and pushed the button for the elevator, Billie looked at their jeans with trepidation. "This place seems awfully fancy for jeans. Are you sure we're not underdressed?"

Jason smiled down at her as he pushed the button for the penthouse. "I'm positive. We're going to my place."

Billie couldn't believe her eyes when they got off the elevator in the penthouse. Besides the beautiful furniture and the panoramic view of the city, there was a low table in the middle of the living room with big pillows around it. It was set for two with china, crystal stemware and linen napkins, and everything looked beautiful There was an appetizing smell coming out of the kitchen and unlike their aborted meal at Pax, Billie was sure there was something really tasty in store for them. She turned to Jason, who had just put away their coats. "Did you cook for me?"

"Yes and no," Jason admitted. "I made the salad, but everything else was catered. They delivered it just before I left and it's in the oven right now."

"It smells wonderful," Billie said appreciatively.

"I can't believe you went to all that trouble for me. Let me wash my hands and I'll help you serve."

"No, you don't. You may certainly wash your hands, but you are to have a seat and allow me to wait on you. I'm trying to impress you and it won't work as well if you're pitching in."

Billie did as she was asked and got a chance to admire Jason's gorgeous marble bathroom while she did so. The tub was big, deep and had a ring of water jets, as well as several shower heads, some mounted and some handheld. She had to tear herself away from the sight because suddenly she wanted nothing more than to strip off her clothes and hop into that magnificent tub.

At last she was seated in the living room where Jason wanted her. He had brought a tray of hot shrimp puffs and stuffed mushrooms, which were delicious. He held one to her lips and she took a bite and smiled in delight. "Jason, these are fabulous. Try one," she insisted, and fed him a shrimp puff the same way he'd fed her. His tongue touched the tip of her finger and she made a little sound of delight.

He looked at her with a knowing expression and said he'd be back with the main course. "Would you like something to drink in the meantime?"

"Yes, I'd love it." When he reached into the ice bucket that was nearby and retrieved a bottle of expensive champagne, Billie cautioned him that she didn't have much of a head for alcohol. "Maybe I should wait until dessert. Otherwise I'll fall asleep on you," she said sheepishly.

"Then I have just the thing," he said. He went into the kitchen and came back with a chilled bottle of lime-flavored Perrier. "How's this?"

Billie beamed and held out her glass, which he filled with a flourish. She took a sip while he cleared the table of the appetizers and returned with a covered tray. He uncovered it to reveal a plump, perfectly roasted capon, tiny red potatoes and crisp green beans. He served her plate, then his. They began eating the moist, tender chicken, and it was soon evident that they could have saved the plates because they ended up feeding each other again. Instead of sitting across from each other, they sat side by side, very close and intimate. It was a lovely meal and Billie was enjoying herself thoroughly. Will Downing's latest CD was playing, there was a fire in the black marble fireplace and everything was romantic and perfect.

Jason wouldn't let her do a thing other than

relax and have a good time, so she did as he asked. He offered her dessert, but she was too full to enjoy it, so he cleared away all the dishes and put the table back in its normal place. Now they were simply sitting on the floor in front of the fireplace, listening to the music and talking. "Would you rather watch a movie? I have everything you can name," he told her.

"We can watch movies anytime," she said. "I'm enjoying our conversation. I can think of one thing I would like, though."

"It's yours," he said at once. "What would you like?"

"Your home is just beautiful, from what I can see. I'd like a tour," she said.

He got up and held out his hand to her. "Let's go."

Chapter 12

Billie and Jason held hands as he started taking her around the penthouse. They started in the kitchen and she was suitably impressed with the expensive appliances and the clever glass-fronted cabinets. She also liked that the washer and dryer were in the kitchen, which was a huge plus in her eyes. Jason put his arms around her waist and said, "If you ever spend the night you could just pop everything in the washer and you wouldn't have to run off first thing in the morning."

She raised a finely arched brow. "You seem to

have given this some thought. Do that often, do you?"

Jason tried to distract her by showing her the pantry. He didn't want to tell her that she was the only woman other than his two sisters, his mother and his assistant who'd ever set foot in his home. He never let any of his women visit because he didn't want them getting comfortable and territorial, but Billie didn't have to know that. They went from the kitchen to the formal dining room, then the study and the exercise room. She was quite impressed and told him how nice it was. The only room left to see was the master bedroom and he threw the door open with a flourish. "This is where I sleep," he said. It was a huge space with impressive floor-to-ceiling windows on two walls. The blinds were pulled and Billie went to look at the view.

"There's a terrace out there. You can go out those doors or the set in the living room," Jason told her.

"That must be nice. Do you spend a lot of time out there?"

"Not really," he admitted. "I always plan to, but I'm always too busy to really kick back, I guess."

Billie murmured, "That's too bad." She turned to face the room with her eyes closed and then

they popped open. She was surveying the room one section at a time. She saw Jason looking at her and she laughed. "I know this looks nuts, but that's how I get the best perspective on things. This is a very stately room, Jason. Very masculine and tasteful," she said thoughtfully. *And very boring and cold. Where is the Jason I know in this hotel suite?* she thought.

She walked around looking at the angular black furniture, the walls covered in blue-gray Ultrasuede and the way the carpet echoed the wall color, only darker. It was top quality Berber and looked very lush. There were brushed-chrome lamps on the dresser and the nightstands and artwork on the walls. The only touch of anything organic was the big potted ficus tree in a corner and she suspected it was silk. Finally there was nothing else to look at but the bed, and what a bed it was. It was big and blocky with a high platform base and a tall, thick, heavy headboard and footboard. It was covered in black leather and probably cost as much as his car. She did like the silk duvet and the pile of pillows, but the bed itself was rather forbidding. Its sheer size was intriguing, however. "That's a big bed, Jason. That might be the biggest bed I've ever seen in my entire life. Did you have it made?"

"Yes, I did." He took a seat on the side of the bed and invited her to try it out. "It's a ridiculous size, but it's the most comfortable bed I've ever slept in." He patted the space next to him and she took him up on his offer. She sat next to him and bounced a couple of times.

"This really is a wonderful bed, Jason. I like it. May I get in it all the way?"

In seconds he'd kicked off his loafers and moved to the head of the bed and was sprawled out like a sultan awaiting his queen. Billie slipped her shoes off and joined him.

"For the record you can get in this bed any time you like," he said. "You don't ever need to ask. Come over here a little closer and let's watch Sports Center. I want to see how bad the Bulls did tonight."

Billie curled up next to Jason and answered yes when he asked her if she was comfortable.

"Very. But I don't see a television. How are we going to watch it?"

He picked up a small remote and pressed a button, causing the large abstract painting on the far wall to split in two, sliding apart to reveal a giant flat-screen plasma TV. He turned it on and tuned it to Sports Center while Billie watched him with interest.

"That is so clever. Don't ever let Nick know about it or he'll have one within two days, which would drive Dakota nuts." She leaned back onto his shoulder and when he put his arm around her a loud "Ouch!" came out of her.

"What's wrong?"

"My earring got caught in your shirt. Ooh!"

"Hold still, sweetheart," he said softly.

"Wait, I've got it," she murmured. She had managed to unhook the earring and sat up, rubbing her earlobe.

Jason looked concerned as he took off his shirt to retrieve the gold hoop earring. "Here it is. I don't think it's broken. How's your ear?"

Billie wasn't listening to him. She was looking at his chiseled chest with avid interest and desire. "My what?"

"Your…never mind," he groaned as he pulled her into his arms. His mouth found hers and there was no more conversation.

Billie sank into the pillows as Jason angled his body over hers. Her hands stroked his shoulders, his taut biceps and his chest. She'd never felt anything as warm and smooth as his skin. His kiss was driving her crazy, the way he was gently

nibbling her lower lip and teasing with his tongue. She murmured his name and he took full advantage by exploring every inch of her willing mouth with skill and unerring accuracy. She was hot all over, so hot and needy that she couldn't breathe properly. She couldn't keep her clothes on another second. If she didn't get them off she would burst into flame, she just knew it. She began to unbutton her shirt and Jason took over when he realized what she was doing. Her white shirt joined his, tossed across the bed. It was nice, feeling the warmth of his hands through the thin lace of her camisole, but it wasn't enough. She wanted to feel more of him.

"Jason, take it off," she whispered.

In seconds the camisole was tossed aside and she felt his skin against hers for the first time. She sighed his name and kissed him again. His fingers found the front clasp of her bra and he undid it in one smooth move. When he slipped it off her body a shudder of pure arousal shook her. It was an amazing sensation that was new to her, but it felt for some reason as natural as breathing. When Jason touched her breasts for the first time, she felt as though he was anchoring her to the bed, because she was floating way

above it. His talented mouth caressed her neck, her shoulder and finally his hot, moist lips surrounded her nipple. This time she cried his name out loud as she tightened her grip on his shoulders.

He continued to apply a sweet hard suction to the sensitive tip that sent her spiraling off into ecstasy. Suddenly he stopped, planting one last kiss on her grateful breast, and then he pulled away.

"Okay, sweetheart, I'll stop."

Billie's eyes flew open and she struggled to sit up in protest. "Oh, no, you won't!" Her eyes were full of reproach and confusion as she stared at him. "Why are you stopping? Am I doing something wrong?"

Jason tried not to smile. Billie couldn't comprehend his expression and repeated her question. "What did I do wrong? I'm new at this, but if I'm not doing it right, just tell me."

His expression changed to one of tenderness, and all amusement left the building. "Billie, baby, you're fine. You're as close to perfection as a woman can be, as a matter of fact. I wanted to stop because I'm guessing you don't have much experience and I didn't want to…ah…"

"Freak me out? Scare me?" Billie looked

directly at Jason and she appeared curious, but not upset or embarrassed. She had no clue how desirable she looked with her glorious hair all messy and her kiss-swollen lips. Jason settled back against the pillows and pulled her back with him, holding her close. He hugged her for a long moment and rubbed his cheek against her fragrant hair.

"Actually, yes, that's about it. I didn't want to scare you. You're doing everything just right, Billie. I'm the one who's messing up. I wasn't wrong in thinking you haven't done much of this, was I?"

"Try *none*. Yes, I have managed to live to this ripe old age and keep the golden snatch intact. I guess I get a gold star or a cookie or something," she said calmly. "And before you ask why, let me explain. As you already know I was not a femme fatale in my younger years. I was a total jock and not very dainty. All my running buddies were guys, and since they thought of me as one of the boys, they (a) never hit on me and (b) used to talk like I was one of them. I heard all the guy talk, so I knew firsthand how they would chase after a girl and beg her like a dog to go out and then swear up and down they loved her. And how they would get the goods and then talk about her like she was

the town tramp. That kept my panties glued to my behind, trust me. I wasn't gonna be the object of locker-room gossip if I could help it."

"But, Billie, after you started modeling and traveling and meeting all those celebrities, you had to have had offers. Come on now, I know you were tempted once or twice."

"Not really. Male models can be absolutely impossible, for one thing. Their egos are mighty fragile and a lot of them are quite confused. They're with a boy one day and a girl the next. Oh, no, thank you to all that," she said, shaking her head. "And please don't get me started on celebrities. I'm a very private person and I didn't want all my business out in the street, something that celebrities by definition thrive on. I was waiting for the right person," she said simply.

Jason was rubbing her flat stomach in slow circles while he kissed her neck. "So why me? Why now?"

Billie stroked his chest and leaned over to kiss the base of his throat. "Why not?" she said mischievously. "I like you, Jason. I care for you and I don't think you're exactly indifferent to me, although I could be wrong. Am I wrong?"

Jason laughed deep in his chest. "I can safely

say that you've never been more right about anything in your life."

"I like being right," she gloated. "So what do we do now?"

He didn't answer; he simply moved her slender body so she was sitting in his lap. "Put your arms around my neck."

"What are we doing, Jason?"

"You'll see. Hold on tight," he instructed, and stood up with Billie cradled in his arms. In less than a minute they were in the bathroom. He set her on the long marble counter and wrapped a towel around her shoulders before turning the water on in the bath enclosure.

"Jason, this looks like fun, but what are we going to do in here?"

He took off his jeans and briefs before giving her a rakish smile. "Everything, baby, everything your heart desires."

Once the water was at the right temperature, Jason turned to Billie and had her stand so she could get out of her jeans. She shimmied out of them and he folded them neatly, placing them on an upholstered bench near the door. She took off the towel he'd given her to keep warm and was

adorned only in her expensive pink bikini panties. When Jason got a look at her he had to turn her around so he could admire every bit of her body. Her legs were long and shapely, her butt was high and firm, and she was just the right height for him. He turned her around so she was standing in front of him while they looked at their reflections in the mirror. He leaned down a little so his head was resting on her shoulder and he slid both his hands down her torso, deftly slipping her panties down until she was as naked as he.

"You're just beautiful, you know that, baby?"

Billie smiled. "You're pretty gorgeous, too. We could be a perfume ad or something. Ever thought about modeling?"

Jason looked horrified at the very idea. "Never. Come with me, sweetheart, I don't want the water to get cold."

"Wait a second," Billie said. She twisted her long hair and swiftly put it into a knot. Then she took his hand and they stepped into the tub. They each took a handheld shower and wet each other thoroughly. Jason picked up a bottle of bath gel that was blue and smelled like the ocean. He poured some into his hand and began to rub it all over Billie's body. He stood behind her and

started with her shoulders, working his way down her arms. After he'd reached her fingertips, he started again, but this time her already sensitive breasts were his target. He rubbed them gently in circles, kneading and caressing them until she had to lean against him for support. His hands went farther, rubbing her stomach and reaching down to the curly mound that covered her femininity. A moan of pleasure was his reward and his fingers parted her thighs and explored the treasure within. He brought her to the edge of fulfillment and then turned her around so he could see the look of abandoned pleasure on her face. She was trembling and her breath was coming in soft little gusts. "Not yet, sweetheart. Hold on for just a minute," he soothed her as he used the handheld shower to rinse her off, and using the spray to bring her even closer to the brink. He put his hands on her hips and kissed his way down her taut body until he was kneeling in front of her. He held her firmly as he kissed her navel before gently parting the curtain of her womanhood and showing her what erotic love was all about.

Moans of pleasure turned into a full-throated cry from Billie and he finally had mercy on her and began to relax his hold as he rose to his feet.

"Hold on, baby," he whispered. "Put your legs around me." She did as he asked and wrapped her long legs around him. He cupped her butt and walked out of the glass enclosure, stopping only to get a bath sheet from the towel warmer. He walked to the bedroom still holding her while he turned the duvet back and spread the towel over the sheets. "Don't move," he said as he sat her on the bed. "I'll be right back."

He was, too, with another large towel. He'd put one around his waist and began stroking her softly with the other one. "Did you like your first lesson?" he asked in a low voice.

Billie smiled a very satisfied smile and said, "Yes, I did. Do I get another one?"

"Absolutely. You're an excellent student," he replied.

"That's only because I have a very good teacher." To his utter surprise, Billie began singing a very sultry version of "Teach Me Tonight."

"You keep singing like that and I'll teach you anything you want to know.'

She grabbed the towel around his waist and pulled it off. Putting both hands around his heavily engorged manhood, she gave him a look that was full of desire and passion but innocent

at the same time. "Teach me what to do with this," she murmured.

He reached for the box of condoms in his nightstand. "It's all yours, baby."

Chapter 13

The next morning Billie's eyes opened slowly. She was wonderfully warm and completely happy. Jason's arm was around her waist and her head was on his shoulder. She rubbed her cheek against his warm skin, wondering how a man so masculine could feel so smooth and soft. The low rumble of his voice made her smile.

"Good morning. Did you sleep well?"

Billie kissed his shoulder. "Good morning to you. I slept like a baby, thank you. You were right, this bed is amazing."

"Forget the bed, sweetheart. *We* were amazing," Jason said with a soft laugh. "No regrets?"

"Don't be crazy," Billie said. "How could I possibly have any regrets?" She had to stop talking because her stomach growled loud and long. "Is there any chance that you didn't hear that?"

"Baby, I not only heard it, I felt it. What would you like for breakfast?"

"Pancakes," she said. "And scrambled eggs and bacon and grits and…"

"I think I have the idea." Jason chuckled. "There's a place not too far from here and I can call in an order."

"I want to cook," Billie informed him. "I want to show off my culinary skills."

"You won't be cooking much of anything if I don't go around the corner and get some milk and eggs. Do you require anything else?"

"Fat-free half-and-half for my coffee. And this," she added as she put one of her long legs over his. "I'm not exactly starving. I can wait a little while to eat."

Jason smiled at her boldness. "Are you trying for extra credit?"

"I just want to be teacher's pet." She giggled.

Jason didn't actually leave for almost an hour.

After making love once more, they took a playful shower together and Jason finally managed to get dressed while they continued to kiss and explore each other. Finally he was fully attired and walking toward the door. Billie walked with him, barefoot and wearing a beautiful, blue silk jacquard robe that belonged to Jason. She had washed her expensive lingerie out by hand the night before, and her shirt and jeans were in the washer on a special steam-and-tumble cycle. She had a toothbrush with her because it was her habit to brush after every meal. Her hair was rather wild, but it looked sexy, as Jason had told her several times. They kissed goodbye at the door like newlyweds and Jason said he'd be back in a few minutes.

"I'm going to make coffee," Billie said.

After the front door closed she went into the kitchen, admiring it again. It was a great space in which to cook, if only she could find everything she needed. She located the expensive coffee-maker and a brand-new bag of Hawaiian Kona coffee beans. "Where there are beans, there must be a grinder," she mused. "But where?"

When the washer signaled the end of its cycle, she took her clothes out and went to the bedroom

to get dressed. While she was in there she removed the sheets and was taking them into the kitchen to launder when the front door opened. A strange man walked into the living room and she froze. Her first instinct was to drop the sheets and grab something to use as a weapon. The stranger evidently knew panic when he saw it, because he held up his hands and spoke in a soothing voice.

"Whoa. I come in peace. I'm not here to harm you or steal something. I'm Todd, Jason's brother."

Billie stared at him. He did sort of resemble Jason, but she wasn't giving in that easily. "Show me photo ID," she snapped.

The man looked amused by her insistence, and when he smiled she knew he had to be related to Jason because their smiles were identical. If it weren't for his long locks, they could have been mistaken for twins. She took the wallet he held out to her and inspected his driver's license and his hospital ID card. Finally she handed it back to him with a smile.

"Sorry about that, but I wasn't expecting you. I'm Billie. Nice to meet you, Todd. Would you like to stay for breakfast?"

"No doubt. I'm always hungry, unlike my Spartan brother. Is he here?"

"He went to the store for milk and eggs so I can make pancakes. I'm showing off for him," she admitted cheerfully. "I make really good pancakes. It's one of my few kitchen skills. Come on in the kitchen," she invited. "I'm also trying to make coffee, but I can't find the grinder for the beans."

"I can help you with that. I know more about his kitchen than he does because I'm always over here mooching." Todd was as good as his word and in a short time the kitchen was filled with the heady aroma of the rich island brew. When Jason returned he was greeted by the sight of his brother sitting on a tall stool watching every move Billie made as she set out cups, saucers and spoons for the coffee. Billie heard him come in and turned to greet him with a smile.

"You're back! We have company," she said.

Jason put the bags on the counter and gave Todd a less-than-friendly look. "I can see that. What are you doing here?" he asked pointedly.

"I'm having breakfast," Todd said smugly. "Billie invited me."

"Consider yourself uninvited," Jason said. "Close the door on your way out."

Billie was looking in various cupboards and not really paying any attention to the men. "Jason, I need a big bowl, a whisk, a measuring cup and a measuring spoon. And do you have a griddle?"

"I'm sure I do, but I have no idea where it might be. I don't really cook that much," he admitted.

"I know where everything is." Todd grinned. "And if I get to eat, I'll get everything out for you."

Billie thought that was a wonderful idea, but Jason didn't look like he shared her opinion.

Despite his initial displeasure at Todd's presence, Jason ending up enjoying the sumptuous breakfast Billie prepared. Her pancakes were light and fluffy and delicious, the turkey bacon was crisp and the scrambled eggs were just right. The three of them had an enjoyable meal with much laughter and good conversation. That alone was a revelation to Jason, who had never brought any of his women around his family. If he ran into Todd at a social event or nightclub he would introduce his lady of the moment, but he couldn't remember ever sitting down like this and sharing a meal or anything close to it. He was completely comfortable with Todd and Billie getting to know

each other. It didn't even bother him when Todd started in on him about his eating habits.

"Billie, you must have worked some magic on him, because he usually has a protein shake for breakfast. Dinner, too," he said, making a face. "Have you ever had one? Well, don't let him make one for you. Whey powder, egg whites, brewer's yeast, fruit and ice cubes. Maybe some razor blades and gravel, too, who knows? You're looking at Mr. Health over there," he said, gesturing at Jason with his coffee cup.

"I'm a different story, however. If it's smaller than me and can't get away, I'll eat it. I have no discrimination whatsoever about what goes in my mouth."

Billie looked at him over the rim of her cup. Her eyes were full of merriment as she asked, "Is that why you complimented my food? Because you'll eat anything since it all tastes the same to you?"

"Aw, no, that's not what I meant. You can really cook, Billie. I was totally sincere when I said it was delicious," he protested. Turning to Jason, he said, "I put my foot in it that time, didn't I? Now what do I do?"

"Make a graceful exit. No, that's not possible. Just say you're sorry and leave—that's probably

your best solution. Get out while the getting is good," Jason said with a grin.

Todd turned to Billie, who was laughing at him. "I really meant it, Billie. You can cook for me anytime. I may be an undiscriminating omnivore, but I know good food when I taste it. But I am gonna get out of here and leave you two alone. It was great meeting you and I hope to see you again soon," he said with a sincere smile.

"You will," Jason said. He was looking at Billie or he'd have seen the pleased look on Todd's face when he heard his brother confirm in two little words that Billie was now a part of his life.

He took his leave of the couple, thanking Billie again for a wonderful meal. Billie was looking around the kitchen to see what needed to be cleaned up. There wasn't much because she was a very tidy cook who washed dishes as she prepared the meal so there wouldn't be a lot to do afterward. "I'm going to get this put away and then you can take me home. I have to help Dakota later on. You're coming to her house for dinner tonight, remember?"

"Of course I do. I'm looking forward to it. But don't you move from that spot. I can get this knocked out in about ten minutes," he told her.

"That's so sweet," she said.

"It's not 'sweet'—it's fair. You knocked yourself out to make me and my brother, the bottomless pit, a wonderful meal. The least I can do is clean up the kitchen."

"Do you really drink protein shakes for breakfast and dinner? What I mean, is that what you normally have? I'm not trying to corrupt you," she said. "I don't eat like this every day, but I was feeling rather celebratory, as well as hungry." She smiled.

Jason continued to tidy the kitchen while he answered her question. "When I was growing up I was a fat kid, Billie. I was a big baby, and then I was a chunky toddler and a plump preschooler. I always had problems with my weight, and since I was the only one in the family who did, it was a real big issue. My mother is a doctor, my father is a doctor and so are my sisters. Todd is a doctor, too. When I was a kid they made my weight seem like it was some kind of rebellion on my part or some kind of failure on theirs. My weight was a huge issue for them, no pun intended. I was still athletic—I played football all through high school and college. But it wasn't until I started my MBA that I really started losing weight," he told her.

"I did it by following a really strict low-carb

diet and exercising. Of course, having a thyroid problem properly diagnosed and treated helped, too," he said with a touch of sarcasm. "So I do follow a pretty strict regime. I work out every day, and other than the occasional lapse into something really delicious like those pancakes, I watch what I eat."

Billie was looking at him with understanding and compassion. "It sounds like you had a lot to deal with growing up. People can be cruel when they're trying to show concern," she said in a soft voice. "But," she said as she got off her stool to walk over and put her arms around him, "if my opinion counts for anything, you've got nothing to worry about now. I happen to know for a fact that you're in excellent shape," she said as she hugged him from behind.

Jason was pleased by her words, but even more pleased by her open display of affection. "So what time is dinner tonight?" He turned around so that he could return her embrace.

"About seven-thirty. I'm not sure what we're having. Probably roast chicken."

"As long as I get you for dessert, I don't care what it is. Are you going to stay with me tonight?"

"No."

Jason pulled away from her so he could look down into her eyes. "Why not?" The words were out before he could censor them.

"Because you're going to stay with me," she whispered.

Jason was amazed at how just a few words from her could make everything feel so right in his world.

Dakota was watching Billie make the giblet gravy for the chicken and dressing. "I may go to my grave without learning how to make decent gravy. What do you do to it that makes it so different from mine?"

Billie laughed. "I make it just like Mama makes hers. Just brown the flour a little, then put in a little butter and the pan juices. Use a whisk to make sure it's smooth and start adding the chicken stock a little at a time. Then, when it starts to get thick, add the chopped liver, some of the meat from the neck and a chopped, hard-boiled egg. Stir it up, put it in a bowl and await applause. It's simple," she said.

"So *you* say," said Dakota. "Personally, it was easier for me to win a Pulitzer than it is for me to make decent lump-free gravy. I've had to resort to buying the kind in the jar and doctoring it up. I feel like such a failure," she said dolefully.

"You really need to quit. Nick didn't marry you for your gravy, honey. He married you because he's crazy about you and he couldn't live without you," she said.

"That's true," Dakota said. "Now what about you and Mr. Gorgeous in the other room? You look pretty taken with him, Billie. And I assume he returns those feelings?" Dakota was smiling, but Billie knew she was as serious as a heart attack.

"Dakota, I don't know how I'm supposed to answer that question. We haven't been involved very long as you already know. And yes, I do have some very intense feelings for him, and as far as I can tell, he feels the same way about me. At least that's what my heart is telling me. Is there a method to use to pry the truth out of him? Some kind of truth serum that I can buy online or something?"

Dakota hugged her sister. "I'm not handling this very well, I know I'm not. But you're my baby sister and I want you to be happy. If there's even the least chance that you could get hurt, I want to prevent it."

Billie hugged her back. "I appreciate your concern and I love it that you're still looking out for me, but you can't protect me from the lumps

and bruises of love. Nobody can. When you fall for somebody you put yourself out there. You open yourself up and sometimes it's wonderful, it's beautiful and perfect like you and Nick."

Dakota nodded. "And sometimes it's complicated like Toni and Zane. She still hasn't figured out that he's in love with her."

"Well, why doesn't he tell her, for heaven's sake? Why is he keeping it such a big secret?" Billie asked impatiently.

"He wants to wait until after she has the baby so she won't feel obligated to him, or some mess. You know how men are—they overthink everything. He should just tell her and she might surprise him, because I think her feelings for him are growing by the day. They'll work it out some way, I know they will," Dakota said. "As soon as the rolls are done we can eat. Tell the fellas to wash their hands and have a seat at the table."

Jason was ready for the inquisition. He'd already answered a lot of questions for Billie's father and he was ready for more of the same from Nick. Nick Hunter was hospitable and friendly, and so was his wife, Dakota. But Jason already had a hint of how close the two sisters

were and how protective Nick was, especially
where his wife was concerned. He figured that at
some point in the evening Nick would pull him
to the side and question him about his intentions
toward Billie.

Sure enough, while Dakota and Billie were in
the kitchen putting the finishing touches on the
meal they were about to share, Nick invited him
into the media room to catch a little of the game.
It was a ruse, of course, but it was as good as any
and he went with Nick into a big room on the first
floor. It held six theater-type chairs that faced an
enormous, wall-mounted, flat-screen television.
Nick turned it on, and offered Jason a drink,
which he refused. The two men sat and without
any small talk, Nick got right down to business.

"Look, Billie is my wife's only sister and that
makes her *my* little sister. She's a real together
lady, real smart, real ambitious and she's traveled
a lot, met a lot of people. But inside she's still a
real down-home girl. She's not the kind of
woman you play with, so if playing is what you
have in mind, we're gonna have a problem.
Billie's a grown woman, but that doesn't mean
you can mistreat her. You probably think I got my
nerve getting all up in your business, but like I

said, that's my little sister and she's very special
to her sister and to me. If you don't plan on
treating her right, I'm gonna have something to
say about it. I just wanted to make sure you understood that," he said with a pleasant smile that was
completely at odds with his tone of voice and the
cool look in his eyes.

Jason's voice was equally controlled when he
replied. "I can understand your concern about
Billie. If she was my sister, I'd be just as vigilant
in looking out for her interests. As you said, she's
special. Actually, that word doesn't even begin to
describe her. She's gorgeous on the outside but
she's uniquely beautiful on the inside. If I thought
I couldn't treat her the way she deserves to be
treated, I'd walk away from her now. But I have
no intention of doing that. You don't have to
worry about Billie while she's with me."

Nick's expression didn't change. "That was a
nice speech. But I only know you by reputation.
Some of it's good, as far as business is concerned.
Some of it's not so good, at least when it comes
to women. But Billie's a pretty good judge of
character and like I said, she's grown. Just treat
her right, that's all I'm saying."

Jason didn't see the point in continuing to go

back and forth with Nick because neither man was going to back down. All he said was, "You can believe the rumors or you can believe me, it's your choice. But you have my word that Billie is not going to have an unhappy day with me."

He was absolutely right in thinking that Nick was going to have the last word. "I'm gonna hold you to that, partner."

Chapter 14

Despite Nick's interrogation and thinly veiled threat to his life, Jason enjoyed the evening with Billie's family immensely. Dakota was warm and welcoming, and as Billie had told him, she was a great cook. The meal of chicken with cornbread dressing, greens and potato salad was one of the best he'd ever had and he'd cleaned his plate with great enjoyment. He normally skipped dessert, but having sampled Billie's pie before, he suspected that Dakota was just as skilled. The hot apple pie à la mode looked and smelled so good he had to indulge. When he remarked that he'd

never had pie that delicious, Dakota proudly told him it was Billie's creation. He hadn't even thought about what he'd done next, which was lean over and give Billie a kiss on the cheek and tell her what a superb cook she was. Luckily no one in the room realized how out of character the gesture was for him.

He was still thinking about that impulsive kiss after dinner was over and he and Billie were back at her home. They were in the living room on the sofa and Billie was curled up next to him trying to get warm. Sadie was cuddled on the other end of the sofa.

"I shouldn't have turned the heat down so low before we left," she said with a shiver. "I wish it would hurry up and get warm already."

Jason's answer to that was to ease her into his lap and cover both of them with the pashmina throw from the back of the sofa. "Is that better?" he asked.

"Mmm, yes," she answered as she snuggled into his warmth. "Come over here, Sadie, so you can stay warm, too, honey. It's a lot colder now than when we left. Are we supposed to have a cold front or something?"

"Some kind of freak storm is on its way," he agreed.

Billie rubbed her nose along his jawline and kissed his cheek. "Did you have fun tonight? I hope Nick wasn't too hard on you. He takes this big-brother thing very seriously," she said before planting another soft wet kiss behind his ear.

"I had a very good time. Nick was just doing what a man is supposed to do, the food was the bomb and your sister is a doll. I didn't get a chance to really talk to them the night of the party, so this was nice. I meant it when I told Dakota I was a big fan. I've read all her books," he murmured while licking Billie's neck. He heard the little sound he was learning to love, a soft little murmur that signaled arousal.

"I'm starting to get warm," she said softly.

"Good. Because once you're nice and warm all over it'll be time for another lesson." His hands slid under her sweater, stroking her soft skin. She turned in his arms until she was facing him and she could wrap both her arms around his neck.

"I'm very warm now," she told him. "And certain parts of me are *hot*." She caught his lower lip in her mouth and sucked on it gently. He returned the gesture and they started kissing in a heated rush of passion.

"Billie, I have to ask you something."

"Anything," she answered breathlessly.

"Where is your bedroom?"

She rose at once and held out her hand. "Come with me." They went to the kitchen first, so Sadie could get on her thick cushion. Then they went upstairs to her bedroom, a cozy feminine oasis. Jason looked around the room while Billie lit several fragrant candles on the dresser, the vanity table and the bedside table. Her room was a marked contrast to Jason's master suite in his penthouse. It was smaller and more intimate and everything reminded him of Billie. The queen-size bed was covered with a quilt that looked handmade. The main colors of peach, green and pink were picked up in other things in the room, like the throw rug on the floor and the curtains.

"Why don't you get comfortable? The bed is smaller than yours but it's very nice," she assured him.

He took off his shoes and sat on the bed, holding his hands out to Billie, who mischievously stayed out of his reach. "Not yet," she said seductively. She took her earrings off and put them in a small glass dish on the dresser. Jason raised an eyebrow and reached for her again. She took another step back and shook her head. "Not

yet," she repeated. She took off her rosy-pink cashmere turtleneck and folded it neatly on the chair in front of the vanity. In her sheer ivory camisole and matching bra, she turned to him and was almost in his arms, but she sidestepped him to turn on the CD player next to the bed. "Almost," she said teasingly as she unfastened her jeans and pushed them down her long legs. Now she was wearing only her underwear and Jason had had all he could take. He stood and put his hands around her waist and picked her up.

She laughed helplessly while he carried her to the bed and put her down. It took him a lot less time to get out of his clothes than it had taken Billie. She barely had time to turn the covers back before he had joined her in the bed. She was still giggling when he rolled on top of her. "Don't play with me, woman. I take this very seriously," he growled.

"Take what seriously?"

"Making love with you," he told her while he removed her delicate camisole. "I have to concentrate on every aspect of it so that I can bring you the most pleasure possible," he murmured as he unfastened her bra and began to feast on her breasts. "I take that very, very seriously."

Billie's face was transformed by her reaction to his touch. Her eyes were closed and her lips were parted in a smile of delight as his mouth worked its magic on her nipples. She could feel his desire for her in the form of his huge, hard erection, and anticipation made her moist and avid for more of him. Her hands caressed his shoulders and her fingers tightened as Jason began taking her to the point where there would be nothing but bliss. He was kissing her stomach now, rubbing his goatee across her sensitive navel and then replacing it with his tongue. She was drifting away as he circled her belly button and lavished it with a long, lingering kiss, but he wasn't nearly finished in his drive to pleasure her.

As he kissed his way down her warm body that was now dewy with the heat of his loving, he slipped her thong panty off her so cleverly she didn't realize he'd done it until his mouth found her most sensitive spot and stimulated it until she was screaming his name. He put her long legs over his shoulders and continued his tender assault on the essence of her womanhood until she was trembling and sighing over and over. Only then did he relent and change positions so that he was on his back with Billie on top of him, trying

to regain control of her senses. He stroked her hair and her back, holding her closely until her breathing returned to normal. He reached over for the packet of condoms he'd left on the table next to the bed and smiled when Billie took it from him.

"It's the least I can do, considering everything you've done for me," she said, giving him a kiss as she removed the packet from his fingers.

She kneeled in front of him on the bed, tearing the packet open carefully. But before she put it on him, she took him in hand and applied a hot, sweet kiss that brought him to an even higher level of arousal. He called her name and she ignored him until he gave a hoarse moan that sounded like a roar. "Billie, sweetheart," he begged.

She relented and raised her head, going back to her original task of rolling the condom onto his hardened shaft. Once that was done Jason surprised her by gripping her hips and guiding her into position on top of him. "New lesson, baby. Have you ever gone horseback riding before?"

Her eyes widened as she felt the length of him in a way she hadn't before. He guided her onto his body and held her tight as she got used to this new position. She rocked against him and they established a rhythm that brought both

of them to shattering satisfaction at the same time. Billie collapsed onto his chest and even in her fevered state she noticed that his heartbeat was as fast and out of control as hers. She moved so that her head was on his shoulder and they held each other until normal speech was possible.

"You aren't still cold, are you?"

Billie gave a soft, sleepy laugh. "Jason, I don't think I'll ever be cold again. Not as long as you hold me like this," she said, just before falling into a deep sleep in his arms.

The next day, Sunday, was unlike any "morning after" in Jason's memory. It was rather remarkable, considering his prolific love life, but what was so striking to Jason was the ease with which he'd slipped into his new role. After he and Billie had awakened and made love again, they had taken a shower before going back to bed wrapped up in each other and nothing else. He wasn't normally a heavy sleeper, but he managed to remain fast asleep until Billie woke him to bring him breakfast in bed. He opened his eyes to find her in the bedroom with a tray in her hands and Sadie at her side. She was wearing a cute peach velour jogging suit, and even

though she wasn't wearing makeup, she looked adorable. "Good morning, Jason. Are you hungry?"

He was at a loss for words. He was so touched by the gesture he couldn't speak, but luckily, Billie kept talking. "Why don't you go brush your teeth or whatever while I set this up for you? I put a toothbrush in there for you. It's blue."

He did as she suggested and went to the bathroom to handle his business. When he came back in the bedroom, Billie had put the tray on the wooden trunk at the foot of the bed and had tidied all the covers. She made him get back under them and fluffed the pillows behind his back before placing the tray in his lap. She curled up next to him and asked if he needed anything else. Sadie lay down next to the bed and looked perfectly content.

"Not a thing, sweetheart. This looks really good. Are we sharing or what?" he asked, seeing as how the tray was set for one.

"Sadie and I ate already," she told him. "I wake up like a ravenous wolverine, so it's best that I eat as soon as possible. I hope you like it."

She'd made him a frittata with diced smoked turkey, red peppers and green onions and low-fat white cheddar cheese. There was also a bowl of

grits, whole-grain toast and her special fat-free hot chocolate, along with a bowl of orange and red grapefruit sections with slices of kiwi fruit. It looked like a spread for a photo in a gourmet magazine and it tasted even better.

"Billie, this is the first time I've ever had breakfast in bed. It was magnificent, too. What can I do to repay you?"

Billie looked offended. "You can stop saying things like that," she scolded him. "In my entire life I've never done anything I didn't want to do and that includes fixing you breakfast," she said with a poke in his hard bicep. She made a move to get out of the bed and he tried to stop her, but the tray was in his way. "Ha-ha, that's what you get," she gloated. She took the tray and told him he had to stay there because his underwear and jeans were in the dryer. "Unless you just want to run around naked," she said suggestively.

"Where are you going?" he demanded. "Aren't you going to keep me company?"

"Not on your life, mister. I'm going to run to the store really fast because I don't want to miss the game. I'll be back soon," she said as she turned to leave the room.

"What am I supposed to do while you're gone?"

"Go back to sleep," she called over her shoulder.

This was so far removed from his normal mode of behavior he had to lie back and think about it. When he was with one of his previous women, he was usually gone from their bed before the crack of dawn. If he happened to spend the entire night with a lady he was out the door before her eyes were open. He wasn't used to this kind of easy-going companionship. Jason didn't often admit it to himself, but he had a basic distrust of the motives of most women, especially the beautiful ones. It stemmed from his "fat boy" childhood.

He crossed his arms behind his head and stared at the ceiling of Billie's bedroom. His first lessons in love had taught him that women were all about looks and loot. If a guy had the right look, he could get laid. And if he had the money, he could get any honey on his arm. After Jason's weight loss he found that he couldn't beat the women off with a club. Especially after he started making bank in real estate. Then he became the object of every woman's desire, but their admiration left him cold. He knew what they wanted from him and he made sure that they got just a taste. He'd dole out just enough for them to know what they'd be missing once he gave them the

Tiffany kiss-off necklace. Now he was in an unfamiliar place emotionally. He didn't know how he'd gotten in so deep with Billie, but he already knew that the same old thing wasn't going to work with her.

He was surprised to find that he actually went to sleep while Billie was out. He awoke sometime after she got back. His clothes were neatly folded on the chest and he could hear music coming from downstairs. He showered and dressed quickly and went downstairs to find Billie. She was in the kitchen preparing something that smelled appetizing and she was singing along with a CD. Sadie was on her cushion and she gave a happy bark when she saw him. He greeted Billie with a kiss and asked what she was making.

"This is my brother's world-famous white-bean chili. It's almost totally fat-free and it's delicious. Since the weather turned so funky I thought this would be good."

Jason hadn't even noticed the weather. He looked out the kitchen window and saw that a healthy snowstorm was going on. "There's nothing like springtime in Chicago," he said. "Do you need some help?"

"Absolutely not. Go turn on the game and just

chill. This has to simmer for a long time after I put it together, so I'll be in there in just a few minutes."

And that was how the rest of the day went. He was sprawled on the sofa all afternoon with Billie lying on top of him when she wasn't stirring the chili. They each had a big bowl of it with piping-hot cornbread and it was better than dining in a five-star restaurant. When it was finally time for him to leave he realized it was the last thing he wanted to do. But he knew Billie had to get some rest because the work on her project started the next day. She wasn't nervous, but she was anxious to begin and she had a lot of things to go over that night. So he reluctantly went home after giving her one last passionate kiss at the door. He was backing the Hummer out of the driveway, and when he looked up to see Billie waving at him, he had to force himself not to stop the car and go right back to her.

Chapter 15

Once the first few days of actual work began on her project house, Billie was sure she'd made the right choice of career. On the first day of "demo," as the demolition phase was referred to, she'd gotten a real charge out of seeing the old cupboards ripped out, as well as the ugly, dated bathroom fixtures. When the wall between the kitchen and family room was cut down, it was plain that she'd made the right design choice, one that was going to make both rooms look larger and brighter. Now, after two weeks of work, the nasty carpet was gone and the hardwood

floors underneath weren't in terrible shape, which meant they could be salvaged at less cost than initially projected. Billie was over the moon and Nick was happy, too.

Nick's crew was handling the general contracting and there would be specialty subcontractors to handle the painting, the floors and the plumbing. Nick was around every day at the beginning of the project, but Billie was in charge, a role she relished. She came home tired and grubby but energized every day. This was her new world and she loved every minute of it, even though it was cutting into her social life. She talked to Jason every day and related her progress.

He gave her encouragement, which she appreciated. He was out of town for two and a half days, and the first night he was gone he told her he missed her and couldn't wait to see her when he got back. It was touching and a little surprising since they had successfully avoided any kind of verbal commitment. But it wasn't so touching that she started asking questions like "Where are we headed in this relationship?" She knew better than that; she'd had an extensive education in the ways of men and how they reacted when they were pinned down. So she just let it flow. She was

satisfied with what they were doing now, whatever it was.

They talked on the phone, he sent flowers and they had dinner together at least once a week. The weekends were just pure passion. He had taken her out to fine restaurants a few times and once to a gallery showing, but for the most part Billie was content to relax at home. They did that a lot and it was her favorite thing to do other than make love. At this particular moment she was glad he wasn't coming back until Friday, because it gave her another day to prepare for his homecoming. She was going to leave work on Thursday and go straight to a spa that had late hours and get the works.

Meanwhile, Jason was fighting fatigue when he got off the plane at O'Hare. He'd had a long workweek and the flight from New York was the last lap in his personal rat race. The conference he'd attended in the city just wasn't all he'd anticipated. The truth was, he just wasn't as receptive to the information as he should have been because he missed Billie so much he couldn't concentrate. It was both humbling and a little scary for him to attempt to assess the impact Billie had on his life. She'd become essential to

him, like air or water or anything else a human required to sustain life.

When he finally made it through the horrible maze that was O'Hare and got to his car in long-term parking, he was tired and irritable. Normally he'd have gone straight home to a hot shower and a cold drink, but he found himself headed to Billie's house with one thought on his mind. He had to see her or he'd never get his head right.

Look at me. I'm like a lovesick kid with his first crush, he thought. He had to laugh at himself. If he didn't know better he'd swear he was falling in love. And if he was, he had no clue about what came next. He was in foreign territory without a map to guide him; no compass to guide him, no market report to study, no statistics for reference. He was a stranger in a strange land.

He pulled into Billie's driveway and felt like he'd reached safe harbor. It exerted a calming effect that lasted up to the point where he rang her bell and a man opened the door. All traces of peace left and a red-hot rage took its place.

"Come on in, man. You must be Jason. I've heard a lot about you," the stranger said.

Jason's mouth was open to say, "I haven't heard a damn thing about you," but he didn't get a

chance. Billie came into the kitchen with her usual smile. "Jason, you're back! This is my big brother, Johnny. Johnny, this is Jason Wainwright."

He shook Johnny's hand, hoping that he didn't look like he felt, which was like the biggest fool in the free world. Now that he was being forced to use basic cognitive reasoning, instead of drawing from some primal wellspring of raw testosterone, he could see a family resemblance. Johnny was his height, a handsome man with the same intelligent eyes as Dakota and Billie.

"Nice to meet you, Johnny. Dakota's told me a lot about you, too," he mumbled.

"Come in and take off your coat," Billie urged. "Johnny is getting ready to go over to Nick and Dakota's house. He's going to be here all weekend—isn't that cool?"

Jason mumbled his agreement. "If you're going to be leaving I need to move my ride," he said. "It's in the way."

Billie was looking at him with concern. "I'll move it, Jason. You go sit down—you look really tired. Did you have a rough flight?" she asked sympathetically.

All at once he realized just how tired he was. He gratefully accepted her offer and went into the

living room to sit. He actually dozed off in the few minutes it took her to back the Hummer out and let Johnny out of the driveway. When she came back into the house he awoke to find her touching his face in concern. "Jason, I think you have a temperature. Come with me, honey. I think you need to go to bed."

They were the sweetest words he'd ever heard in his life.

The next few hours were rough for Jason. Billie was right when she said he had a fever; he'd been burning up, in fact. She had gotten him undressed and in the bed, but in about a half hour he was in the bathroom. He was normally the picture of health, but he'd gotten a killer flu bug that didn't want to let go. His head ached, his body hurt and he couldn't keep anything in his stomach. If he hadn't felt so lousy he would have been embarrassed to let anyone see him in this condition, especially Billie, but he had no say in the matter. Billie had taken over and she didn't appear to be fazed by his condition. She seemed to know just what to do for him.

She'd put him to bed and kept him covered up, even when he was hot. It was good that she did,

because he was roasting one minute and freezing the next. She brought him ginger ale and chipped ice; she rubbed his feet and put hot cloths on his forehead to relieve his headache. She called Todd to see if there was anything else she could be doing, and he said he'd bring him medicine and something for nausea. When he arrived, Billie met him downstairs and took him up to check on Jason.

He came back down and reported that it was the flu, as she'd suspected. "There's been a pretty nasty strain of it this year. You're lucky to have avoided it yourself."

"I had a flu shot," Billie told him. "I hate being sick so I do everything I can to avoid it."

"Normally Jason does, too, but I think he's just a little run-down. He works too hard," Todd said. "You're good for him, Billie. You are really good for him. You're the first woman he's ever been with who cared about him just for him and not for what he could do for them."

Billie looked surprised by his words. "But how can that be, Todd? He's so wonderful," she said with obvious sincerity. "He's so kind and funny and thoughtful—how could someone not see that?"

Todd hesitated a moment and then plunged ahead. "You have to understand that Jason had it

tough when he was growing up. Do you know what his nickname was? Porky," he said sadly. "And that was his *family* nickname. I never called him that because he was my big brother and we always had each other's backs, but other people could be quite nasty. My parents made a huge deal out of him being overweight. He caught hell at home and at school. Then after he lost weight and turned into the Jason you know now, the chicks that had been dissing him all his life suddenly saw him as the perfect catch. He'd never tell you this, and I probably shouldn't, either, but that's the story. Anyway, I'm glad that he found you. You're just what he needs in his life."

Billie quickly replied that he was what had been missing in *her* life. "Jason is…everything to me," she said. She looked at the bottle of pills in her hand. "How long will it take these to work?"

"A few hours will show a big difference. You're doing a great job, though. If you weren't so gorgeous and talented in other areas, you might have made a great doctor," he said.

"Uh, no thanks," she said, shaking her head. "I can't stand to see anyone in pain. When can he start eating?"

"Whenever he can tolerate it you can start

feeding him. Start him out with gelatin and clear broth, and when he's had enough of that he'll let you know." He walked to the back door with his arm around Billie's shoulders. "I'll check in on you every so often. Call me if you need me."

· Billie spent the night dozing next to Jason and was gratified when his fever finally broke. The next day she kept him supplied with liquids when he wasn't sleeping, which he did a lot of because of the medicine for the nausea. And when he finally started spending more time awake than asleep, she started him on gelatin, chicken broth and Popsicles. He was a surprisingly good patient, which pleased Billie to no end.

"I thought sick people were supposed to be grouchy," she said. "I'll take care of you anytime, Jason. You're the perfect patient." Sadie put her head on the side of the bed as if to agree with Billie.

"That's only because you're so good to me. I can't remember the last time I was sick, but I know I didn't get all the TLC I'm getting now. I've got a comfortable bed and a grape Popsicle. Who could ask for anything more?" he said with a smile. "Not to mention my two beautiful nurses. Has Sadie been up here all the time?"

"Yes, she has. She's been keeping an eye on

you. Don't forget the Gatorade," she reminded him. "As much as you want. Are you hungry yet?"

"Not really," he said, rubbing his stomach. "What day is it?"

"It's just Saturday afternoon. The worst of it was last night, but the medicine Todd brought you really helped."

"I still can't remember him being here. I must have really been out of it."

"You were, but you're much better now. Why don't you get some sleep and I'll go make you some chicken soup for later?"

"Stay with me awhile. You need some rest, too. I don't want *you* getting sick."

"Honey, I'm made of iron. You don't have to worry about me," she said. But she stayed with him just the same, waiting until his even breathing told her he was asleep before she slipped out of bed. She kissed him on the forehead and went downstairs to make soup.

By Monday Jason was well enough to go home, even if Billie insisted that he take another day off before going to work. "You should probably take off Tuesday, too. You don't want to have a relapse," she said firmly.

Jason was feeling mellow enough to agree.

"I'm going to work from home for a couple of days. But you have to promise to take a day off, too. You wore yourself out looking after me."

Billie looked tempted but wouldn't promise. "There's so much going on at the house I can't take a break. I'll be doing good to make it to lunch with Toni and Dakota on Tuesday. We're making wedding plans for her and Zane. But if it starts raining real bad this week, I'll have a day off because we're getting the roof done and you can't do it with rain pouring down. So keep your fingers crossed for bad weather." She laughed.

Billie did make it to lunch with her sister and her friend on Tuesday. In deference to her working attire of jeans and work boots, they picked a deli not too far from her work site. Toni and Dakota looked like ladies of style and she looked like a construction worker, but it didn't bother her a bit. She hugged them both and sat down at the table. "Who's got a menu? I'm starving."

Toni gave them a sheepish smile. "You know I really appreciate you wanting to do this for me, but I keep telling you we can go to Vegas this weekend and get hitched, no problem."

"Oh, no, you're not," Dakota said quickly.

"You're getting married the same place I did, in my living room. You're not going to skulk off and get hitched in some tacky little rhinestone chapel. You're going to have a nice little ceremony and a nice little reception afterward. Don't argue with me," she warned.

Toni's eyes teared up and she apologized. "I'm sorry but I'm like a leaky faucet these days. I can't seem to keep the waterworks turned off." She sniffled. "Thanks so much, Dakota. I don't know what I'd do without you two."

Billie patted her hand. "And you won't have to find out. We need to eat fast because I've got to get back to the site. And pray for rain so I get a free day this week. We've got a wedding to plan!"

Chapter 16

The only thing Billie couldn't figure out later was why Dakota hadn't told Toni that Zane was crazy about her. It made no sense to her that Dakota would withhold that kind of vital information. "You know Zane is nuts about her. Why don't you tell her so?"

"Because one thing I've learned over the years is how to mind my own business, baby sister. He'll let her know in his own way when the time is right. You don't want to see her go into information overload at this stage. We could have a runaway bride on our hands if he springs some-

thing like that on her now. It will all work out, trust me," Dakota said.

"You certainly sound like you know what you're talking about. I'll defer to your superior knowledge in this case, but I have to say if it was me, I'd want to know," Billie said.

"Saying those magic words isn't as easy as you might think," Dakota said sagely. "Have you told Jason that you're in love with him?"

They were on their way to see the progress that had been taking place on the project house, and Billie almost went off the road when Dakota asked her innocent little question. "No, I haven't told him! And if you want to get to the house in one piece, I suggest you not drop a bomb on me like that. You're gonna get us killed out here."

Dakota just laughed at her. "I struck a nerve, didn't I? What are you waiting for? You know you love him. Just go ahead and get it all out—you'll feel better," she teased. "And if it'll make you feel any better, I was the one who said the words to Nick first."

Billie was immediately interested. "Did you really? Weren't you scared?"

"Not at all. I was in love, that's what I was. But with Nick, it was just so easy to fall in love with

him. He was my man and he knew it before I did. He never held back from me and he made it so easy for me to give him my heart," she said with her usual dreamy-eyed, Nick look.

Billie was happy to pull up next to the Dumpster in the yard. "Yeah, you and Nick are my ideal romance," she said. "But Jason and I, well, I don't know where we are in the romance ratings. He's sweet and sexy and he treats me like a queen," she said as she got out of the car. "And yes, I'm totally in love with him, like that's a big secret. But as far as any passionate declarations, there haven't been any. None of that 'You're my woman' stuff from Mr. Wainwright, nope, not at all." She was trying to sound light-hearted but she didn't quite succeed.

Dakota linked her arm in Billie's as they picked their way across the wet lawn. "I wasn't trying to make you feel bad, honey. I was just playing. Your relationship with Jason is nobody's business but yours and you don't have to explain it or analyze it for anyone, including your nosy older sister. Whether he says it or not, Jason is crazy about you and if he treats you well and appreciates the wonderful person that you are, that's all that matters."

They were in the house now and Dakota looked around with wonder. "This hardly looks like the same place! You're on a roll here, girl. This is amazing," she said. "Now that those hideous curtains and that smelly carpet are gone you can see the possibilities. Billie, you're going to be really successful one day and it's all because you have real vision. I'm so proud of you!"

Billie accepted her praise with her usual modesty. "It's because I've learned so much from Nick and because I've been blessed with great workers. I love doing this, Dakota, and I'd like to do it for the rest of my life. And some big bucks wouldn't hurt, either."

They looked around the house one last time before going off to shop for the wedding. They were looking for dresses to wear. Toni had already selected her dress and she really didn't want Dakota and Billie to go to the expense of buying something new, but the sisters wouldn't hear of it. "Any occasion that calls for a new dress is a friend of mine," Dakota had told her.

Billie was a great shopper but she really only enjoyed it when she was doing for other people. But this time she was looking for something special because Jason would see her in it, and she

wanted to knock him out. She always wanted to look her best when she was with him, and she couldn't say why this was so important, but it was. Neither she nor Dakota wanted to look like traditional bridesmaids and they both wanted something they could wear again, so they avoided the bridal shops and headed for an upscale boutique that Toni had told Dakota about. Dakota found something right away in a pretty shade of peach. It fit her perfectly and showed off her curves beautifully with its long sleeves and deep, draped neckline. The skirt was knee-length, so Nick would get a good look at her legs, which he loved.

It took Billie a little longer to find her dress, but it was a great find indeed. It was short, like Dakota's dress, but it was a deeper shade of peach and it was strapless. It was simple and elegant, skimming her body and showing off her long legs. She loved the way it looked and couldn't wait till Jason saw her at Toni's wedding. He always liked seeing her dressed up and told her so often. Since his recovery from the flu they'd been out a few times, always to someplace very upscale and posh. He might not have declared it himself, but there was some comfort in the fact that he liked to be seen with her. They made

a stupendous-looking couple if she had to say so herself. And one day they might be even more to each other. Only time would tell.

Jason could count on one hand the number of weddings he'd attended. He had nothing against the institution for other people, but he'd never considered himself a candidate. Many women had tried to drag him along to their sister's wedding, their best friend's or cousin's weddings or whatever, but it never worked. He knew that women got overly romantic and caught up in other people's weddings and he wasn't trying to give out any false hope. However, when Billie invited him to Toni and Zane's wedding, it didn't occur to him to say no. He'd go anywhere Billie wanted him to go, even if it was to a tractor pull.

He'd known for some time that he had strong feelings for Billie, feelings that were far more intense than he'd ever had for any other woman. But after the loving way she took care of him when he had the flu, he knew two things. One was that he was in love with her, and two, that she was the only woman he could ever love. Billie was everything any man could want and that she cared for him too still amazed him.

He knew she loved him; he had no doubt of that at all. She was so caring, so unaffected and open with her affection that she couldn't have hidden her feelings if she tried. Luckily for him, she never tried. What you saw was what you got with Billie. And he wanted all of her for all time, which was why he was going to propose.

When he told Todd what he was going to do, he thought his brother was going to pass out.

"You're gonna what?" Todd yelled.

They were having lunch in a sports bar when Jason made his announcement. "Man, use your inside voice—we're not at home," Jason said with a laugh.

"Hey, you can't drop a bomb on me like that and not expect me to react. You're actually gonna do the deed, huh? You got a ring and everything?"

Jason nodded. "It's beautiful. And before you ask, no, it didn't come from Tiffany's. It's really gorgeous, though. It's going to look good on her hand."

"So when are you going to pop the question? I do get to be best man, right?" Todd looked like he was willing to debate the issue if Jason said no.

"I'm trying to wait until after the house is done

so we can concentrate on us. She's so busy with her renovation she doesn't have time for too much else, and I don't want to distract her. But get this—it's been going so well she'll have it wrapped up next week, two weeks ahead of schedule. My baby knows what she's doing," he said proudly.

"She'd better if she's going to marry you. She has to know what she's getting into," Todd joked.

"Just for that, you can pick up the tab, Slappy."

Todd was so elated he didn't care. He'd just won a bet with himself, that Jason would be married to Billie before year's end.

Nick and Dakota's house looked lovely. Because the wedding was so small, with just Nick and Dakota standing up for the couple and Jason and Billie as witnesses, they held the ceremony in the solarium. It was full of flowers and candlelight and it was the perfect place for them to exchange vows. Toni was a gorgeous bride in a blush-pink silk dress with three-quarter-length sleeves and a scoop neck. It fell just below the knee and it had a subtle empire waist that emphasized her still-small waistline and camouflaged the tiny baby bump. She looked radiant, and if

Billie didn't know the circumstances, she would have thought they were just a couple in love.

Billie didn't know how Toni could have been unaware of Zane's feelings for her; he was looking at her with eyes so full of love it was almost blinding. But she also saw a look on Toni's face that looked very much like a reflection of Zane's, so maybe Dakota was once again totally correct and things would be working out just perfectly. She certainly hoped so, because nothing would be more wonderful than to see Toni as happy as Dakota.

After the ceremony, there was a nice dinner from Toni's favorite restaurant and a lot of pleasant conversation and relaxation. There were wedding gifts, too, which made Toni cry. Zane had the pleasure of kissing his bride's tears away. All in all, it was a perfect day. Billie would remember it for a long time because it was going to be the last happy day she had for a while.

She and Jason went to his penthouse for the night. Her dress had the desired effect on him and he couldn't wait to take it off. Their lovemaking was hot, feverish and full of passion, as it always was. Afterward, though, Jason surprised her. He always had some kind of surprise for her,

whether it was flowers or a massage or perfume or something else he'd thought she'd like. This time, though, he surprised her with a question. They were in the Jacuzzi enjoying the whirlpool when he asked her if she planned on getting married.

Her eyes widened and she looked closely at him to see if he was kidding. He looked perfectly serious and so was she when she answered. "Yes, I do," she said firmly. "I want to get married and have children, at least two, preferably four. Why do you ask?"

"Because I want to know if you're the settling-down type or the kind of lady who plans to be independent all her life," he said.

"But you should already know that," she said, and splashed water in his direction.

"Just because I'm sure of something doesn't mean I don't want to hear it confirmed," he said. "Now I'm going to confirm something else," he said. "I'm going to show you how long I can hold my breath underwater. Come here, baby."

If the evening had ended with them sound asleep, she might never have seen the so-called entertainment news show on late-night cable. But after some more energetic lovemaking they

decided they were thirsty and Jason went into the kitchen to make them frozen raspberry margaritas. She turned on the television and there was some kind of voyeuristic talk show about toxic bachelors or something. She was about to change the channel when the overly animated female host said, "But look out, ladies! These lethal Lotharios aren't located just on the east or west coasts. Any of you beauties in the Windy City need to look out for Jason Wainwright, the real-estate whiz. This man goes through women so fast they don't even have time to register on his caller ID, honey." A barrage of clips of Jason with other women sped past and ended with Jason being interviewed about his playboy reputation.

He was on a long sofa and the same beady-eyed woman was sitting next to him looking like she was trying to dump her cleavage into his lap. "So tell me, Jason, why is it you can't seem to settle down with one lady?"

"Why should I?" he said with a smirk. "There are just too many of you lovely women out there and I can't disappoint you, now, can I? That's why I have to stay single so I can mingle with all of you." He grinned.

"When do you think you'll settle down?" she asked archly.

"Bring the camera in for a close-up so everybody gets the same message," he invited. And there was the face she'd grown to love leering at the whole world as he mouthed the word *never.* "Got that? I'm never tying myself down to one woman. Not gonna happen, not in this life."

Then the woman came back onscreen with what she called an update. "You fashionistas out there know the fabulous Wilhelmina, right? Well, apparently she's Mr. Wainwright's current piece of arm candy." A series of shots of her and Jason at the gallery opening, at a concert and even at his black tie gala where they'd originally met paraded across the screen, and Billie had to fight not to throw up.

"Somebody needs to tell Ms. Girlfriend that being six feet tall and drop-dead gorgeous isn't enough to keep that lover man interested for more than two months, tops. She'll be replaced soon if she hasn't already."

Billie was fully dressed by the time Jason came back to the bedroom with their drinks. "What's the matter? Where are you going?"

"I'm getting out before you kick me out. I just saw your interview on that odious talk

show," she said as she pointed to the TV, "and it was most illuminating."

"What interview? What are you talking about?" Jason looked genuinely confused.

"Did you or did you not do an interview for a TV show about why you'd never get married?" she demanded angrily.

"Oh, that. It was a long time ago, Billie. It was just a fluff piece, it meant nothing," he began, only to be cut off.

"It couldn't have been that long ago because they had footage of me in it, Jason. There were pictures of you and me as your latest piece of arm candy, as she referred to me. She also had a friendly warning for me. She told me not to get comfortable because I was about to be dropped. How do you think that made me feel?"

"It shouldn't have made you feel like anything," Jason retorted. "It was a bunch of junk, Billie, and any fool should be able to see that." He set the tray down on the dresser and walked toward her, but she moved away from him.

"Well, I must be a new kind of fool because I couldn't see it. I saw me on the show being made into a joke on national television and the sight made me sick. I'm getting out of here, Jason.

Goodbye and good luck with your next piece,"
she said viciously before she walked out of the
bedroom and out of his life.

Chapter 17

Billie had always been a Christian, but now she was sure there was a heaven and a hell. There had to be because she'd been residing on the seventh level of hell since the day she'd stormed out of Jason's apartment. She'd spent a good part of every day since in tears or near tears, and they showed no signs of flagging. Thank God she had a sister like Dakota. She knew exactly what Billie was going through, because she'd experienced the same thing with Nick the previous year. Dakota and Nick were engaged to be married when Dakota had let herself believe a

huge lie that his ex-wife had cooked up and she broke things off with him. She'd been just as miserable as Billie was now and she offered up ample sympathy.

"Look, honey lamb, just go ahead and bawl your head off, but when you get done, you call Jason up and get him to talk to you. You can work this out," she said soothingly.

They were sitting in Dakota's kitchen, which was full of sunshine and a complete contrast to the way Billie was feeling. "You tried to talk to Nick after you two had that blowup and he wouldn't listen to you," she mumbled.

"Well, yeah, but maybe Jason isn't as stubborn as Nick. And remember, I saw that same show and I was just as hostile as you were. How were we supposed to know it was originally telecast two years ago with the new footage cut in so they could recycle their mess? I guess we're going to have to start watching more junk TV," she said, rubbing Billie's arm.

"Or stop watching it altogether," Billie said glumly. "This is one of the reasons I stopped modeling, because I can't stand all that gossip and lies and innuendoes and crap that goes along with being a so-called public figure. I was just trying to

make some big bucks to start a business. I wasn't trying to be in the damn limelight." She sniffed.

"Have you heard anything at all from Jason?"

"Not a word. Would *you* call me after I talked to you like I talked to him?" She paused to blow her nose and looked at Dakota quizzically. "Did I say that right?"

"Yes, you did. I knew just what you meant, honey. Why don't you call him?"

Another tear trickled down her cheek. "Because I'm afraid of what he's going to say to me," she admitted. "As long as I don't hear anything it's not over. I know that's crazy, but that's who I am these days. A stomp-down, bona fide, certified, blubbering nitwit, at your service," she said bitterly.

"Cut that out! Your project was finished ahead of schedule and you already sold the house! That's not the work of anybody's nitwit. Everybody's entitled to make a few mistakes in life and in love and you just made yours. Call him, honey. What's the worst that could happen?"

She got up to answer the phone and Billie continued to sit at the table, brooding. Nick came into the kitchen and saw her looking like death eating a soda cracker and shook his head. He sat down with her and turned her head to face him.

"I can't have my baby sister being so miserable. It's not good for you, darlin'. You want me to go get him for you?"

Billie's eyes went from weepy to alarmed and she shook her head furiously. "No, Nick, please don't! He didn't do anything wrong—it was all me. I'm the one who jumped to conclusions. I'm the one who acted like a fool. It wasn't anything Jason did. It was my fault."

Nick looked totally serious. "Well, it seems like if you broke it you're the one who's got to fix it. I always thought you Phillips women could do anything. You're lettin' me down, Billie. Worse than that, you're letting yourself down and Jason, too, if I'm not mistaken. I told him what I'd do to him if he messed over you. Maybe I should have given you a little warning, too."

Her face turned pale and she put both hands to her face. "Nick, I can't believe what a wuss I've been. You're absolutely right. I've let both of us down and I've got to fix it." She jumped up from the table and kissed him on the cheek. "Tell Dakota I'll call her later."

Dakota came back into the kitchen to see Billie flying out the back door. She stared at Nick in amazement. "What did you do?"

"What I do best—I talked sense to her. Come kiss me, woman, I'm lonely," he growled.

"You won't be for long," she cooed. "We're going to have company pretty soon," she said.

Nick frowned. "Who's coming here?"

"I don't know for sure. Either your son or your daughter, I can't say for sure right now."

Nick grabbed her and there was no more talking to be heard for quite a while.

Billie took Nick's advice to heart. The only thing that kept her from going straight to Jason's apartment that very moment was the fact that she looked like fresh hell. That, plus it was Saturday morning and she had no way of knowing where he might be. It would serve her right if he was with some other woman, someone who wasn't as spiteful and jealous as she was. She went to her town house and took a shower, then applied her makeup with the speed she'd learned backstage when she'd modeled during Fashion Week in New York. In about an hour she was lotioned and perfumed from head to toe, her hair was curled and she was looking like she was on her way to a red-carpet event, although her attire was a lot more

casual. She had on a black miniskirt, her favorite sling-back platform shoes, and a bronze
leather jacket that matched her bronze DKNY
bag. When in doubt, look fabulous, that was
her motto.

She was taking her heart in her hands and
giving it to Jason. Whether he wanted it or not was
another story, but she wouldn't know if she didn't
try. She tried parking in the visitors' lot of Jason's
building but it was full, so she had to park several
blocks away. She didn't mind because it gave her
another chance to clear her head and rehearse what
she was going to say to him, that is, if he deigned
to let her in at all. She walked like the model she
was, her long, runway stride catching the attention
of every man within a one-block radius. A fashion-
director friend of hers had always teased her by
saying, "You need to look out, girl. Those legs
could stop traffic." She'd always found it hilarious,
but like so many things in life it came back to bite
her in the butt at the worst time.

She was at the intersection of Lakeshore Drive
and another very busy street and the traffic light
changed to green, but the taxi that sent her sprawl-
ing didn't seem to see the red light that should
have made him stop. She went from being a

stone-cold fox to being knocked out cold on the street in less than ten seconds.

Jason was pounding away on the punching bag in his exercise room. He was concentrating completely on the precise repetition of punches and almost didn't hear the phone. He stilled the bag and snatched up the phone, his impatience clear in his voice. "Yeah?"

It was Todd, sounding oddly subdued. "Jason, you need to come over here now," he said.

"Come where, Todd? To your place?"

"No, Jason, come to the hospital. I'm at work and they just brought Billie in. She's been in an accident."

Jason didn't even stop to shower. He did manage to put on some sweats over his gym shorts, and he grabbed a jacket on his way out the door, but his whole being was focused on getting to Billie. Todd was an emergency-care doctor at Cook County Hospital and Jason thanked God that he'd been on duty when she was brought in. He got there as fast as possible and went to the desk to have the nurse on duty page Todd. It wasn't necessary because Todd was waiting for him. He took Jason to the cubicle where Billie

was being held, but before he pulled the curtain back he warned him.

"Jason, she's got a bad bump on the head and she has a concussion, but she's fine. She's probably asleep because I gave her something for pain." Todd had to touch his shoulder. "Are you listening to me? Do you hear me?"

"Yeah, I hear you. Just let me see her," he said.

Her face was pale and there was a big bandage on her forehead and to Jason she looked incredibly weak. She was sound asleep and he couldn't resist touching her cheek. She murmured something and he managed to sit in the chair next to her bed. Todd had followed him into the cubicle.

"It looks worse than it is, Jason. We'll probably keep her overnight just to make sure she's okay, but she'll be fine." He looked at his brother and grinned. "Are we gonna have to keep you, too, Slappy? You look worse than she does."

"Laugh it up, jerk. That's not *your* woman lying there. Are you sure she's okay? She looks really weak to me."

Todd assured him she was fine. "Why don't you go call her sister and then you can come back and sit with her until we get a room ready upstairs? It's fine, Jason. I told you it looks a lot worse than it is."

Jason ignored him and leaned over the bed to whisper in Billie's ear. He'd never felt so useless in his entire life. There was one thing he could do and he did it. He called Dakota's number and was relieved when Nick answered the phone. "Nick, this is Jason. You need to bring Dakota down to Cook County Hospital. Billie's been in an accident. She's fine, she just got a bump on the head, but they want to keep her overnight and I know Dakota would want to be here."

Nick thanked him and said they'd be there immediately. Jason went back to Billie's bedside to wait for her to wake up.

Billie was so tired and so sleepy. People kept calling her name and she wished with all her heart that they would shut up. *Jason should make them be quiet,* she thought. Jason didn't bother her like that. He only said sweet things to her and he didn't pester her like these strangers. He loved her and wanted to make her happy and they were going to be married.

"Billie, come on, Billie, we know you're in there. Come on, Billie, you can do it, honey. Open those eyes, honey."

Finally Billie couldn't hold out any longer. "If

I do will you please shut up?" She blinked her eyes and stared into the brown eyes of a stranger. "Who are you?" She didn't mean to be rude, but she'd never seen the woman before. Her eyes roamed around the room, which looked completely unfamiliar. "Where am I?"

Luckily the woman didn't seem offended. "*There* you are, sugar. It's about time. You've had some people worried about you," she said. "You're in the hospital."

"Really? Why?" Billie's voice sounded croaky and her throat was dry. "May I have some water?"

"You don't remember anything, do you, sugar? Well, your fiancé is here and your sister is on her way back over. He'll explain everything to you. I'm Sarah Johnson, the charge nurse. Your doctor will be in with your fiancé in just a minute."

Billie had a slight headache and there were a couple of places on her body that felt a little sore, but she couldn't understand why she was in the hospital of all places. The door to her room opened and in walked Jason with a bouquet of tulips and a medium-size black woman in a white lab coat.

"Jason, why am I here?" was the first thing that popped out of her mouth.

He came around the bed and leaned over to

kiss her on the cheek. "You were in an accident, Billie. Do you remember anything about it?"

She thought as hard as she could. "No. How long have I been here?"

"I'm Dr. Lomax, Billie. Let me ask *you* a couple of questions. What day is it?"

Billie thought again. "Saturday."

"Close but no cigar, dear. Today is Sunday. Your accident was on Saturday. You were crossing the street on Saturday and you were hit by a taxicab. Do you remember anything about that?"

Billie winced as Dr. Lomax shone a pinpoint of light into each of her eyes. "No, I really don't. When can I go home?"

"Today. Your fiancé will give you more details when you're not feeling so fuzzy—how does that sound?"

After the doctor left, Jason pulled up a chair next to the bed on what Billie had figured out was her good side. "Jason, I'm confused. And my head hurts. Why do people keep calling you my fiancé?"

"Because I told everyone that I am," he said. "How do you feel?"

"Pretty sore in places. Pretty good in others. Why did you tell people we're engaged?"

"Because I love you and I intend to marry you

as soon as humanly possible. Would you like to see your ring?"

"Sure," she said eagerly.

He reached into his pocket and pulled out the biggest ring Billie had ever seen. "Wow," she said. "That's really pretty."

He thought she was dozing off again but she kept talking. "I love you, too. Can we get married tomorrow?"

"Maybe not that fast, but it'll be really soon, okay?"

"Mm-hmm," she murmured, and this time she did go back to sleep.

Much later that day, she was much more alert and things started to come back into focus. With Nick and Dakota's help she was able to piece together the events of the day before her accident, although she still couldn't remember being hit. "It's probably for the best," she said, making a face. She tried teasing Jason about it, but he wasn't ready to joke about something that could have taken her away from him forever.

"I was coming over to throw myself at your feet and beg forgiveness," she said playfully. "I came to my senses and I realized what an idiot I'd been."

Jason didn't smile a bit when she said that.

"You didn't owe me an apology. I was the one who was acting like a fool."

Billie's eyes filled with tears and she wiped them away hastily. "I still owe you an apology," she whispered.

"I owe *you* one. I should have never let you leave angry. I should have made you listen to my heart, baby."

Nick had had enough of the two of them. "You both owe me because I talked sense into her. You can pay us back by babysitting, how's that?"

Billie laughed. "Well, as soon as you have something for us to sit, I'm sure it won't be a problem."

Dakota grinned. "In that case, you'll be real busy in about seven months. Six and a half, actually."

Billie looked at Dakota, then at Nick and then understanding dawned. "Oh, snap! I get to be an auntie and a bride in the same year. I can't wait to get out of here and do a happy dance," she said. "And I don't want a small, tasteful wedding, either. I want a big mamma-jamma wedding with the works!" she said firmly.

"Sounds like a plan to me. As long as we get our honeymoon in Bali, that is," Jason replied.

They were kissing so passionately they never heard Dakota and Nick leave the room.

Chapter 18

The wedding that Billie wanted usually took a year to plan, but with lots of help from her mother and the best wedding planner in Chicago, the nuptials were set for November. Most brides would have turned into bridezillas during the planning process, but Billie was calm and happy. She admitted freely it was because of all the help she had gotten.

"I'm not kidding myself," she told Dakota as they began to get ready to leave for the hotel. "If I hadn't had you and Toni and Ayanna and Patsy helping me, I'd have probably lost my mind. But this has all been just fun for me."

Dakota rubbed the burgeoning belly that would soon produce her son or daughter and smiled. "Even meeting your in-laws? Are you telling me that was fun?"

Billie made a horrible face as she paused to make sure that she had everything she needed in the valise she was taking with her. "Okay, so that part wasn't fun. No, honey, I'm not about to tell you a lie like that. I'm just amazed that Jason and Todd turned out as well as they did, because their sisters are absolute snots!" she said emphatically. "And his parents, well, let's just say I've met some cold fish before, but those two take the proverbial cake. Thank God they live in New York," she added. "If I had to see them more than once a year, it could get ugly, trust me."

Billie had met her in-laws in the summer and even though they had been cordial, she hadn't felt any real affection. His father, John, and his mother, Muriel, were very formal people who seemed distant and cold to Billie. And his sisters, Davina and Cloris, were just utter pills. They were both very attractive but terribly impressed with themselves. They talked about nothing but their medical practice, something that came off as pretentious and slightly pathetic to Billie.

"I was really trying to get to know them better. I did the right thing and asked them to be in the wedding. It's not my fault they turned me down," she said cheerfully.

"I still can't believe they actually asked you who was designing the dresses! When you told them you were wearing the Mizrahi collection from Target I thought they were going to pass out." Dakota laughed. "That was so wrong of you. It saved you a whole bunch of trouble, but it was wrong and you know it."

"Hey, there's nothing wrong with those gowns at Target. They're well made and beautiful and a good price. Can I help it if one of my best friends happens to be one of the best-known designers in the world? And the fact that he designed all the gowns is something they'll find out today with everyone else," Billie said smugly.

Lee called upstairs to let them know that the limo had arrived, and all conversation came to a halt. Billie raced down the stairs with Dakota following much more slowly, as befitted a pregnant woman. The limo would take them to the hotel where all the bridesmaids would gather to be coiffed and made up by another of Billie's dear friends from her modeling days. Lee hurried them out the door.

"Come on, ladies, time's a-wastin'. Billie, you look less like a bride than anybody I've ever seen in my life," she chided her.

It was true; Billie was wearing jeans and a sweatshirt that read "The future Mrs. Jason Wainwright," which had been a shower gift. "Aw, Mama, I don't look that bad. In an hour or so I'll be good, just wait," she promised. "The next time you see me I'll be ready to walk down the aisle and you'll be bawling your eyes out, watch and see." She hugged her mother tightly and kissed her hard before dashing out to the waiting limo.

Jason was in the same hotel and he was relaxed and calm, something that was a big disappointment to Todd. "You really let me down, Slappy. I was hoping you'd be pacing around like a crazy man, sweatin' and salivatin'. Here you sit all cool, calm and collected. This is all wrong," he said with disgust. "I had a whole bunch of jokes to make at your expense and now I can't use them."

"Don't worry about it, Slappy. They won't go to waste, because one of these days you might find a woman who can tolerate you and I can torment *you* on your wedding day. But for now,

you need to rest your nerves and learn from the master," Jason said lazily.

He was lying on the bed propped up on pillows with his arms crossed behind his head. All the groomsmen, who included Nick, Paul, Johnny, two of Jason's cousins and two of his best friends from college, were dressed. Jason was the last one to don his tuxedo, but it was all good. He wasn't nervous about getting married to the woman of his dreams, but he was really, really anxious for the ceremony to start. He couldn't wait to see his bride and know they'd be together forever. Todd suddenly loomed over him, tapping his index finger on his watch crystal.

"Do you plan to get married in your bathrobe? If you do, just keep lying there. If not, get dressed."

Nick and Johnny concurred. "Last thing you wanna do is be late for a Phillips woman. You better get dressed pretty soon or risk her wrath," Nick warned.

Johnny said, "If you want to enjoy your honeymoon you won't want to be late for the ceremony. Billie can hold a grudge when she wants to." He laughed.

Jason got up with a smile on his face. "I was waiting because I didn't want you all to feel bad

when you see how fine I'm going to look in my tuxedo. You all look good," he assured them. "But I'm gonna look better," he boasted. All the men groaned as he preened in the mirror.

Todd picked up a bottle of water with a squirt top and aimed it at the tux, which was hanging on the closet door. "Say what?" he drawled.

At last Jason's suave demeanor vanished and a look of pure panic swept over his face. "Don't play," Jason warned him.

Todd was grinning from ear to ear. "Gotcha, Slappy." Everybody roared with laughter and even Jason had to join in.

A hush fell over the church as the last chords of the violin and piano duet played by Ayanna's nephews faded away. The minister emerged from a side room and ascended to the pulpit, followed by Jason and Todd. They looked magnificent in black tuxedos with white shirts, gold waistcoats and rosebuds in their lapels. The music began again and the doors to the sanctuary opened. The wedding party entered in pairs.

All the dresses were in the same eye-catching silk fabric, a gold-suffused shade of deep orange that shimmered in the candlelight. The front of

Model Perfect Passion

the church was filled with candles and there were tall candelabras on either side of the aisle. Each dress was made to fit the woman who was wearing it, so each one was unique. They carried bouquets of birds-of-paradise that looked fantastic with the gowns. They all looked beautiful as they took their places at the front.

A soft murmur came from the guests as Dakota entered on Nick's arm, followed by Toni on Zane's. It was unusual to have two matrons of honor and even more unusual for both of them to be pregnant, but this wasn't a run-of-the-mill wedding. Their gowns, like Billie's and the other bridesmaids, had been designed by her friend Taylor Rodriquez and made specifically to complement their rounded bellies while accentuating their beauty. Poor Toni was so close to delivery that she had to wear a pair of flip-flops because her feet wouldn't fit into anything else, but she was determined to walk down the aisle. And the shoes were gold with sequins, so they still looked cute.

The flower girls were next, in delightful peach-colored dresses. They were the daughters of one of Billie's friends from her modeling days. She now had two lines of clothing, as well as a line of cosmetics and her own television show, and

she was one of the bridesmaids, too. Most of the guests recognized the little beauties from seeing them in ads and modeling with their mother, so a buzz went through the church as they walked daintily and sedately to the front, sprinkling gilded rose petals as they walked. Ayanna's nephews followed them, unrolling the traditional white carpet for the bride. Now it was time for Billie to enter.

Everyone stood and turned to the back to see the doors open to reveal Billie on the arm of her father. She seemed to float in her gown, which was a work of art. It was a soft, candlelight white with a subtle gold sheen. The bodice was strapless, sprinkled with tiny fourteen-karat gold beads and the back dipped almost to the waist. The skirt was pencil slim with a bouffant beaded overskirt in the back that led into a long train. It was simple, elegant and very sexy.

The front of her hair was pulled up and back into an elegant topknot above a cascade of waves that came down to her shoulder blades. Roxanna Maxey, makeup artist to the stars, had done her makeup in a way that made her look like a doll come to life. Billie knew she'd never looked better. Her only jewelry was a pair of brilliantly

sparkling pearl earrings with dangling pear-shaped diamonds, a gift from Jason, along with the diamond-and-pearl bracelet on her arm. She carried a bouquet of Tropicana roses, the same as the buds in the men's lapels. The rich coral color of the roses was perfect with the bridesmaids' dresses.

Boyd walked Billie to the end of the aisle and Jason came to claim her from there. Before he released his youngest daughter, Boyd said a few words in Jason's ear. Jason solemnly shook the older man's hand before taking Billie the rest of the way to the altar. Billie's eyes were shining with love as she looked at Jason. There were a few tears as Johnny and Dakota sang "The Lord's Prayer" and "You and I." When they exchanged their vows, Billie had to blink back tears and her voice was full of emotion, but Jason's voice was loud and sure as he took her to be his wife.

He took both her hands in his and kissed each one of them before bending his head to claim the first kiss of their married life. It was a moment that neither of them would forget as long as they lived. She turned to him as they walked down the aisle after the ceremony.

"That was fun. Can we go on our honeymoon now?"

He laughed. "The rest of our life together is going to be a honeymoon. Right now we're going to party, because if we skip out on the reception your momma will flip out."

Billie giggled. "Well, we'll just put in an appearance and skip out early, okay?"

"Anything you want, any way you want it, baby. That's what I'm giving you from now on," he vowed.

"I'm going to hold you to that. And I'm going to do the same for you," she promised. "I love you, Jason."

"And I love you," he whispered as he pulled her into his arms. The receiving line could wait.

Epilogue

Jason kissed Billie's long neck while he held her close to his chest. They were both nude, but it didn't matter because they were in the secluded and very private thatched pavilion that was attached to their honeymoon cottage in Bali. He finally stopped kissing her long enough to speak. "That sunset reminds me of our wedding," he murmured.

The colors of the sunset were like the brilliant hues of the bridesmaids' dresses. Billie kissed his chest before answering. "You noticed? I'm really impressed. Most men don't pay any attention to

the wedding—they're just relieved it's all over," she said with a soft laugh.

"That's because I'm not an ordinary man, baby," Jason growled. "When are you going to figure that out?"

Billie felt his manhood growing against her stomach and sighed with pleasure. "You've got me convinced. Let's go inside."

He picked her up and carried her into the lush, seductive suite with its view of the ocean. "I remember every detail of our wedding. It was the best day of my life."

"Probably because you had the most fun of anyone there," she teased him. "I thought we were only going to stay a little while."

Jason laughed and rolled over on his side to face Billie. "Yeah, but who knew that we were gonna party like that?"

Jason had broken his promise to Billie, but it couldn't be helped. The reception was so much fun they couldn't leave. The music was wonderful, the food was exquisite and everyone was dancing and partying so hearty that it just wasn't possible to make an early departure. Billie and Jason's first dance was to "So Amazing" by Luther Vandross, followed by a dance with the

entire wedding party to "No Diggity." Everyone was clapping and cheering as they did a stylized number that looked like a music video.

Even Jason's normally formal parents loosened up and hit the dance floor with everyone else. Billie's family and friends were so lively and so much fun that the Wainwrights joined right in. Jason's sisters were so awed by the splendid gathering that it was plain they regretted turning down her request to be bridesmaids.

"Cloris came up to me and asked where I'd gotten my dress. She said it looked like a Taylor Rodriquez knockoff. Unfortunately Taylor was standing behind her and tapped her on the shoulder. He said, 'Honey, you should learn more about fashion. This is a Taylor Rodriquez original, unlike that Versace knockoff you're wearing.' I thought she was going to sink through the floor!" Billie's eyes crinkled with merriment at the memory.

Jason snorted. "I have a feeling they're going to be your new best friends, now that they realize you know everybody in the civilized world. When they find out our wedding is going to be in *Vogue, Essence, People* and *InStyle,* they're gonna freak out. They'll be coming to visit every other week or so."

"Please, say it isn't so," she groaned. "I don't want a lot of company. I just want to be alone with my husband."

"Yeah, but we're going to have a lot of room for guests," Jason said with a mysterious sparkle in his eyes.

"Where are we going to put guests? There's not that much room in your penthouse," Billie said.

"*Our* penthouse," he corrected her. "Yeah, but there's plenty of room in our new house. Well, there will be once you're finished rehabbing it."

Billie sat up with huge, excited eyes. "What house?"

Jason reached under the pillow and handed her a small album with about ten pictures of a huge brick mansion. "Your other wedding gift. If you don't like it, we can keep looking, but I thought you'd like the challenge of making this into our dream house," he said, his voice low and sexy.

"Jason, I love it. I love you. I love this honeymoon," she said, wiping away tears of joy. "We're going to have a wonderful life together, aren't we?"

"And you know this," Jason affirmed. "Now

put down those pictures and let's see if we can make a baby before we go home."

Billie let out a happy giggle that was drowned in the passion of his kiss.

A steamy new novel from *Essence* Bestselling Author

GWYNNE FORSTER

DRIVE ME

Wild

Reporter J. L. Whitehead would do anything for
a story—even pose as a chauffeur to newly made
millionairess Gina Harkness. But when business
turns to mind-blowing pleasure, will Gina believe
that though J. L.'s identity is a lie, their untamed
passion is real?

**"SWEPT AWAY proves that Ms. Forster
is still at the top of the romance game."**
—*Romantic Times BOOKreviews*

Coming the first week of April wherever books are sold.

KIMANI™
ROMANCE

www.kimanipress.com

KPGF0600408

She dishes out advice…
but can she take it?

Dear Rita

Favorite author

TAYLOR
Simona

On paper, Rita Steadman's antiman advice column
convinces Dorian Black they're a match made in hell.
In person, though, desire keeps drawing them together.
Add danger to the mix in the form of a stalker,
and the sparks really fly!

**"Taylor has a superb flair for developing
drama and romance."**
—*Romantic Times BOOKreviews*
on *Love Me All the Way*

Coming the first week of April wherever books are sold.

KIMANI
ROMANCE
™

www.kimanipress.com

KPST0620408

From the acclaimed author of
STRAIGHT TO THE HEART...

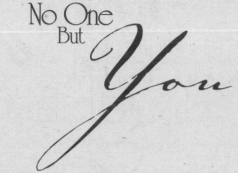

No One But You

MICHELLE MONKOU

Jackson Thomas knows he was a fool years ago to choose his family's business over Sarafina Lovell. Now he intends to win her back with lots of sweet, sensual loving...and a little help from her friends, the Ladies of Distinction.

"Sweet Surrender (4 Stars)...is an engaging love story."—Romantic Times BOOKreviews

Coming the first week of April wherever books are sold.

KIMANI™
ROMANCE

www.kimanipress.com

KPMM0630408

"Never again will I hold onto a Kim Louise book. As soon as it reaches my hot little hands, I will find the quietest spot in my house and lose myself in her work."
—RAWSISTAZ Reviewers on A LOVE OF THEIR OWN

National bestselling author

KIM LOUISE

Sweet LIKE Honey

When Honey Ambrose's online sex-toy business takes off, her brother hires professional organizer Houston Pace to help her out. But when Houston arrogantly insists that anyone who needs gadgets doesn't know what they're doing in bed, Honey takes matters—and her toys—into her own hands....

Coming the first week of April wherever books are sold.

ARABESQUE®

www.kimanipress.com

KPKL0700408

*A tangled web of revenge,
deception and desire…*

defenseless

National bestselling author

ADRIANNE
byrd

Beautiful Atlanta ad exec Sonya Walters knows her sister's
marriage is in trouble. But when her brother-in-law is
murdered and her sister is the prime suspect, Sonya
turns to the one man who can help—defense attorney
Dwayne Hamilton. Sonya is determined to keep things
purely professional…but soon finds herself defenseless
against Dwayne's seduction.

"Byrd proves once again that she's a wonderful storyteller."
—*Romantic Times BOOKreviews*
on THE BEAUTIFUL ONES

Coming the first week of April wherever books are sold.

ARABESQUE®

www.kimanipress.com

KPAB0810408

Three powerful stories of
mothers, daughters, faith
and forgiveness.

BESTSELLING AUTHORS
STACY HAWKINS ADAMS
KENDRA NORMAN-BELLAMY
LINDA HUDSON-SMITH

This Far by *Faith*

The relationships between three women and their
mothers are explored in this inspirational anthology.
As secrets and lies are brought to light, each must
learn about redeeming faith, the power of
forgiveness and enduring love.

*Coming the first week of April
wherever books are sold.*

www.kimanipress.com   KPANTHOL0240408

Books by Melanie Schuster

Kimani Romance

Working Man
Model Perfect Passion

Kimani Arabesque

Lucky in Love
Candlelight and You
"Wait for Love"
Until the End of Time
My One and Only Love
Let It Be Me

A Merry Little Christmas
Something to Talk About
A Fool for You
You Never Know
"Chain of Fools"
The Closer I get to You

MELANIE SCHUSTER

started reading when she was four and believes that's why she's a writer today. She was always fascinated with books and loved telling stories. From the time she was very small she wanted to be a writer. She fell in love with romances when she began reading the ones her mother would bring home. She would go to any store that sold paperbacks and load up! When she had a spare moment she was reading. Schuster loves romance because it's always so hopeful. Despite the harsh realities of life, romance always brings to mind the wonderful, exciting adventure of falling in love and meeting your soul mate. She believes in love and romance with all her heart. She finds fulfillment in writing stories about compelling couples who find true, lasting love in the face of all the obstacles out there. She hopes all of her readers find their true love. If they've already been lucky enough to find love, she hopes that they never forget what it felt like to fall in love.

"What does a brother have to do to meet you?" Jason said with a debonair smile.

Billie raised an eyebrow and hesitated a second before extending her hand for a shake.

"All you have to do is say hello. I'm Billie Phillips." There was a gleam in his eye that she couldn't quite interpret and she waited to see what he would say next.

Jason brought her hand to his lips for a brief kiss and missed the look on Billie's face when he said in a low, silky voice, "It's a pleasure to meet you, Wilhelmina. I'm surprised to see one of the most sought-after models in the world at my event."

"My name is Billie," she said firmly. "Wilhelmina is the woman they pay to pose. Billie is the real person."

She waited for Jason's reaction. Some people got it right away that she wasn't trying to trade on her reputation. Other people took longer to catch on. And some people never got it. Billie hoped Jason Wainwright wasn't one of the clueless ones!